D0612224

TO LOVE A COWBOY

Laura Phillips

A KISMET™ Romance

METEOR PUBLISHING CORPORATION
Bensalem, Pennsylvania

First Printing February 1992.

ISBN: 1-878702-78-5

Printed in the United States of America

To Alfie, Karen, Mary, and
Sally, for everything.

LAURA PHILLIPS

Laura Phillips is a former reporter and news editor who began writing fiction after her first child was born. She lives in Kansas City, Missouri, with her husband, three children, and assorted pets. When she isn't writing or doing Mommy jobs, she can be found in the backyard garden.

Other books by Laura Phillips:

No. 22 *NEVER LET GO*
No. 40 *CATCH A RISING STAR*

ONE

It was just your imagination. It wasn't her. It's been ten years since you've seen her. She's probably fat as a cow, married with six kids by now.

Dipping a finger into one of the pots of greasepaint, Nick Ramsey smeared a wide band of red around his mouth. He tried to forget about the eerie tingle that danced up his spine when he saw the black-haired woman over by the concession stand a little while ago.

He paused to glance out the dust-fogged window. Damn! Still no sign of Matt or the horses. He shifted positions, easing the dull ache in his leg.

"Where the hell is Matt?" grumbled the small, lean-framed woman seated across from him at the dime-size table. Freda Millikan crunched viciously on the stale popcorn.

"It's not my day to watch him," Nick answered mildly, ignoring her bad mood.

"Somebody needs to," Nick thought he heard her say before she jammed more popcorn into her mouth. "Got any chocolate?"

The last bit came through loud and clear, alerting Nick to the fact that Freda was more than irritated. She was ready for the kill. He put aside all thoughts of the black-haired woman.

"Fresh out," he muttered, wishing he'd had the sense to drag Matt along with him on that side trip four days ago. If he had, he wouldn't be having mental visions of wrong turns, highway pile-ups or of Matt and that redhead from Cheyenne curled up together somewhere, oblivious to passing time. That last thought irritated Nick, but not half as much as he suspected it irritated Freda.

Usually, Nick and Matt traveled together. Nick pulled the horse trailer behind his battered black pickup truck, while Matt pulled the gooseneck camper with his newer red pickup. Sometimes they competed in the rodeos, either to settle in one of Nick's horses or just for the fun of it. Mostly they concentrated on rodeo bullfighting.

It was a semi-insane way to make a living, Nick thought, between the constant traveling and the sheer danger of it. Then again, he'd saved the life of more than one friend.

But now they were back in Kansas, and Nick had wanted to drop by the farm for a few days between bookings. Matt had taken the horses and swung north to a rodeo at Sweet Springs. They'd agreed to meet here this afternoon, a couple of hours before the rodeo started. And Matt was very late.

Nick glanced out the window at the empty space beside the trailer. Then the woman's steady, suspicious gaze caught his eye.

"You know something, and you're not telling me," she accused.

"Nope. And quit staring. You'd think you'd never seen a man put on makeup before," he said, trying to distract her.

She quirked a pale eyebrow before she spoke. "I

haven't. You two tough cowboys work your horses all day until you're covered with horse sweat and manure. Then you step into this trailer and lock the door—"

"We don't lock the door," he interrupted.

"Yes, you do."

"Only sometimes. Matt's afraid you'll catch him in his underwear."

"Hah!" she retorted, and Nick raised a brow of his own. Freda grinned. "None of your business," she added, then tossed a kernel of popcorn into the air, catching it neatly in her mouth. She tried it again, but it bounced off her short-cropped, dark-blond head. She scrunched up her freckled nose and leaned closer, focusing those sharp brown eyes on something in the vicinity of his nose until he glanced irritably in the mirror to see what was wrong.

"I like that shade," Freda quipped. "It looks good on you. Of course, since we have about the same coloring, it probably would look good on me, too. Maybe you'd let me borrow it sometime." She struggled to maintain a straight face as she dipped a finger in the direction of the red greasepaint, then dodged Nick's slapping hand.

"Brat," was all he said as he wiped his fingers on a rag, then reached for the white greasepaint. At least he'd succeeded in distracting her, he thought as he proceeded to apply the rest of his makeup.

A full thirty seconds passed before Freda's control collapsed and a stream of laughter bubbled forth.

Nick glared. "Now what?"

"You look like a giant pair of lips."

"Funny, huh?"

She nodded, giggling. "Very funny. Now I know why you guys never let me watch you get ready."

"You won't again if you don't shut up," he replied, his mild tone softening the words to a gentle tease.

The three of them went back a long way—him, Freda, and Matt. They'd called themselves the three caballeros at one time in the distant past when their parents had been the competitors and they'd been three, tag-along kids.

A few years later, he and Matt had graduated from spectators to card-carrying Professional Rodeo Cowboy Association competitors. Both rode the bulls, or tried to. Neither could stay on the full eight seconds that entire year.

Not content with sitting on the sidelines, Freda had shown up the following summer with a fast, tight-turning mare that gave a few more experienced barrel racers plenty to worry about. The following year, Freda was among the top five money winners in her event, and she'd stayed on top since.

The two boys hadn't done as well as Freda, but they'd made a respectable showing, enough to keep them in gas money, but not much else. It wasn't until they met up with a certain rodeo clown that they began to make a living from another side of the bull riding business. He gave them a few tips and hired them to tell corny jokes and keep the audience entertained while he got on with the serious business of keeping Brahman bulls from mashing the riders to a pulp. In time, the roles were reversed. Eventually, when old injuries and arthritis sapped his speed and agility, the old clown retired and left Matt and Nick to find their own bookings.

And now, Matt had better show up soon or Nick would be working this one alone. He would do it if he had to, but he didn't like facing a two-ton bull without a good barrel man. Besides that, Matt had the horses. And that presented a few more problems.

"You don't suppose he had an accident?" Freda asked, a thread of tension creeping back into her voice.

"Naw. He probably stopped at some truck stop and flirted too long with the waitress."

Typical Matt, her answering smirk seemed to say.

Picking up a thick black grease pencil, Nick outlined the smile, then added the marks of perpetually surprised glee at his eyes. Staring at his reflection in the lighted mirror, he smoothed out a smudge in his makeup, then flexed his exaggerated brows.

"Well?" he asked.

"Nice, but something's missing. You could use a touch of mascara." She winked and backed toward the door, dodging the empty paper cup Nick threw. "I think I'd better go change clothes and get Lady Jane saddled up," she added, and ducked out the door.

Nick glanced back into the mirror. Mascara? Forget it. He looked goofy enough already.

But something was missing, something besides his partner. The thickly penciled black brows drew together as he frowned and considered. It wasn't just that he was worried about Matt. The light buzz of anticipation, of energy singing in his limbs, hadn't begun. At first, it had hit in the middle of the night before a rodeo, waking him from a restless sleep. As the years passed and his experience melded with already quick instincts, the buzz had held off until a few hours before the rodeo. Sometimes now, he didn't feel it until the bull and rider left the chute. Even then, there was no edge of sense-heightening fear, except when he felt the bull's hot breath on his neck or the not-so-light brush of one of those deadly horns.

He was tired. Not from lack of sleep, though that could be responsible for the rough edges around his manner lately. He just needed a break—a few weeks, not a few days. Life on the road, day after day, month after month, was grueling. It wore at your reserves until you had nothing left to run on but the caffeine from that morning's coffee.

Behind him the door squeaked open, then snapped shut with a light click.

"I was beginning to think you got lost," he said when Matt crowded past him. The wiry, mustached man began stripping off clothes, flinging them to the floor.

"I did," Matt answered as he pulled on a fringed shirt, hot pink boxer shorts, suspenders, and a pair of breakaway overalls. "I was thinking about something else, and I went the wrong way on Highway 54. I ended up at the river before I realized it. How much time do we have?"

" 'Bout half an hour before the show opens, then another fifteen minutes or so before the bulls." Nick didn't ask what Matt had been thinking about. He had an idea, but he didn't want to talk about it, not now when Freda might pop back in without warning.

"Freda was just in here looking for you," Nick said, with a hint of warning in his voice.

"Yeah, I know," Matt answered with an exaggerated wince. "She had a few choice words for me when I left the bay mare over at her trailer. By the way, that bulldogger from Austin is warming up the black out in the field. He said he already arranged with you to use him tonight."

Nick nodded, feeling the tension in his shoulders ease at the mention of the horses. "We talked about it a few days ago. Where's the truck?"

"The rig's out in the field where they're parking cars. I'll move it after the rodeo, after the place clears out a bit. It was easier to park it and walk the horses in than to try and drive through that crowd. How's the leg?"

"Just fine," Nick said, turning away. It ached, but

not worse than yesterday or any other time in the last two weeks since he'd strained the ligament. Not much better, either.

Ten minutes later, he'd stretched out and jogged around the section where the campers and horse trailers were parked. Then he and Matt made their way over to the arena to await the end of the wild cow-milking contest. Although most of the men in the arena were locals, he recognized a few boys from the circuit, kids who still had more guts than sense.

Then the pickup men were herding the cattle out a gate at the far end of the arena while the announcer explained that the bull-riding would be held in two heats, one now and one at the end of the rodeo.

Nick nodded when Matt lifted his arm and signaled for a conference in the middle of the dirt arena. Nick stepped backward, away from the chutes. He walked with a loose, aimless gait that belied the coiled tension, the surging adrenaline that kept his senses at a high pitch.

The crowd at the twenty-third annual Benton Arena Rodeo had quieted to a low buzz. Even in the relative safety of the bleachers, there was a hum of tension, of anticipation. Excitement with a capital E.

Well, they'd get it, Nick thought. The last bull of this heat was up next, a huge, twisting monster by the name of Devil Eater. Nick almost pitied the pale, determined kid who straddled the fence next to the chute while he and the other cowboys adjusted the wrap of the rope. The bull lurched hard against the gate, and the men fell back, cursing as the rope slipped to the ground beneath the bull's feet.

Nick moved to fill the time until the rider was ready. About ten feet from Matt, he faked a stumble and dropped to the ground, distracting the crowd from the morass at the chute.

"Watch where you're goin', ya cock-eyed idiot," Matt shouted, kicking over the padded barrel and rolling it to where Nick lay. He stopped once to glance around, and his multicolored wig slipped sideways.

"Hey, Nick," he whispered sotto voce while the rodeo announcer joined in on the act. "I found a ringer for the bra routine. You see that black-haired doll over there by the fence? The one with the camera?"

Lifting his head, Nick squinted down the length of the dirt arena, following the comic tilt of his partner's painted face. The bra trick was a simple and well-worn one, but a guaranteed crowd-pleaser. And Matt had added a few twists of his own to the old standard.

Then he spotted Matt's ringer, or rather, spotted the glint of reflected light off the camera lens. *Her.* The woman who had looked so much like a girl he used to know that he'd lost his breath for a minute. Then he'd noticed the sleek, sophisticated differences.

"Third fencepost, sitting with that white-haired guy? Bad choice, Matt." Nick reached out and jerked Matt's feet from under him so that he landed hard and rolled with the barrel while the crowd roared with laughter. Then Nick hoisted himself to his feet with exaggerated effort and helped to right the barrel.

Matt popped out of the top, aimed a phony punch at Nick's nose, and came away with red greasepaint on his knuckles. "Ooops. Sorry," he said as Nick grabbed his ear and twisted a bit harder than necessary in retaliation for the miscalculation.

"Hey, action in the chute," Matt interrupted, and the announcer dropped his straight-man act to describe Tornado, the next bull that was about to emerge. The two clowns moved forward with Nick in the lead, instantly shedding the slapstick act.

Rocking on the balls of his feet, Nick flexed his calf muscles, then stretched. The ache in his ankle had returned earlier than usual tonight. Nick gritted his teeth, flexed the ankle again, then tried to push the pain from his mind. He couldn't afford the distraction. He could tell that Matt noticed, but then not much slipped passed him when they were in the arena. That was the one thing Nick *could* depend on.

"That black-haired sweetheart took my picture a minute ago," Matt said. "Probably works for the paper here. I think she'd be a good sport," he said, positioning the barrel and bracing himself inside. "Tornado'll lead left out of chute. Two spins then back to the right."

"Three spins. And her father might not be," Nick argued, his eyes darting to the woman, then back to the chute where the massive gray Brahman bull kicked angrily at the barrier.

Then the gate swung wide and the beast charged, bucking the wild-eyed youth off with the first bounce. Nick swished close, distracting the bull from the scrambling body beneath his hooves. Nick whirled and slid past, then ran for the open space with the bull fast on his heels. He dodged, then herded the bull through the side gate to the pens.

As he turned around, he caught Matt's signal to begin the bra routine, and he groaned aloud. The woman's camera came down, and Nick glimpsed her face before Matt stepped in the way.

Black hair and big eyes. Exotic eyes that would be black as ink when he got close enough to see them. Slim and sophisticated and as self-contained as he'd ever seen. City polish and shine. *Not her after all*, he noted with a hint of disappointment. And he realized then that he'd like to know how that bright, day-dreaming girl who'd tugged at his teenage heart had turned out.

TWO

"Craig, why did I let you talk me into this?" Melody Williams murmured to the man crouched beside her at the woven wire fence that separated the audience from the action at the Benton arena. She'd canceled two dates, one for a rock concert and another for dinner theater, all because Craig insisted he needed her. So now she was breathing dust and sweating in some out of the way Kansas town. There wasn't even a highway within five miles.

"I'm a silver-tongued devil, and you can't resist me," Craig replied with a wink. "Can't help but love me, can you, Dee?"

Taking her eyes from the viewfinder for an instant, she aimed a sneer in his direction. "After this? You'd better aim your blarney at Mom from now on, old man."

"Ouch!" He winced, but Dee didn't believe for an instant she'd hurt him. She'd known Craig since she was in college and sat through the course he taught in children's literature. After she changed her major from education to art, he'd helped her see the connection between the two. Since then, a good portion of her work as a free-lance artist had included illustrations for various children's magazines and a few picture books. And somewhere along the line they'd gone from their student-mentor relationship to become good friends. Craig was practically family. Dee suspected he'd like to make the relationship official, and she wouldn't mind having him for a stepfather. But her mother was dragging her feet.

His next words proved he hadn't taken her criticism seriously. "You know, you owe me for this one. I had to practically twist my publisher's arm to let you do the illustrations for my book. He wanted some New York fool to do it. The guy probably wouldn't know a Stetson from a bowler."

"That may be true," Dee answered. "But I'd like to remind you that I'm not enjoying this."

Craig looked puzzled. "I figured you would. Your mother said you used to."

She simply grunted and focused the zoom lens on the clowns. She'd better stop brooding and start taking pictures or she'd have nothing to work from but her memory when she started sketching. The voice over the loudspeaker announced the kids' calf roping contest, and the clowns started another string of loud, bad jokes to fill the time between the events. Then one of the clowns walked her way and shouted something that caught her attention.

"I think he's talking to you," Craig said. "He wants you to come closer."

"No way. I'm not about to be the butt of some corny, and probably sexist, joke. I didn't fall for that when I was a kid, and I'm sure not going to fall for it now." Dee tugged at Craig's arm, propelling him backward to the safety of their seats on the front row of the bleachers.

The other clown shouted something, and a loud argument ensued as the two buffoons traded wife and mother insults. Then, to her horror, the one with the strangely colored hair started to climb the fence. The smiling one tapped him on the back, whispered something, then took the place of the first. He scaled the fence and leaped to the ground, landing directly in front of her. He looked her square in the face and grinned wider.

"Oh, no," she whispered and grabbed Craig's arm. "Not me. Take this old guy," she said more loudly. Craig only laughed when the clown shook his head and leaned closer to Dee.

She glared up at the man and braced herself, wondering just what he intended to do. Something in her expression must have warned him, because he hesitated. "Unbelievable," he said, barely loud enough for her to hear him. "Gray and green."

"What?" she exclaimed, thrown off balance by the hesitation. His uncertain brown eyes slowly deepened in color, staring into hers with simmering heat. Serious eyes at an unserious moment.

He brushed back her feathery bangs and stared at the scar on her forehead. She was so surprised, she didn't even try to stop him.

"Good Lord, it *is* you," he said in a faint voice not at all in keeping with the bright, happy paint on his face. He shook his head, as if to clear away the cobwebs. Then he seemed to step back into character.

"Ain't she a purty one," he yelled to the crowd in that section of the bleachers. He planted a loud kiss on her cheek before pulling a huge purse from under his shirt.

"Got it," he shouted to his partner and headed back over the fence.

"Oh, no," Dee muttered, letting the camera drop unheeded to her lap. "I think I'm going to be sick."

Craig wiped tears of mirth from his eyes. "That wasn't so bad, was it?" he said when he'd recovered enough to talk.

"It's not over yet," she said, glaring into the arena at the crowing clown who was refusing to obey the announcer's order to return the allegedly stolen purse. When he pulled a giant, hot-pink pair of panties from the bag, she groaned. The biggest bra she'd ever seen followed. Craig burst into a new fit of laughter when the clown squeezed the hot-pink confection and a horn blasted.

"See? Do you really think I wanted to be a part of that?" she said. "The jokes haven't changed in twenty years."

"You're not old enough to remember twenty-year-old jokes," Craig retorted as he struggled to regain control of himself.

"Believe me, I remember all of it only too well. I don't miss it a bit. Especially not now."

She didn't, she told herself. Not the jokes and not the horses or the tight little world that welcomed no outsiders. You can't turn back time, and for that Melody was infinitely grateful. Not for anything would she relive those horrible years of her adolescence, espccially the three years on her stepfather's farm. Her *ex*-stepfather now. She didn't even like thinking about it, but the smell of manure and all those horses and pointed-toed boots on bow-legged cowboys couldn't help but remind her. She was still an outsider. She still didn't fit in. Only now it didn't matter, she reminded herself.

"Surely it wasn't that bad," Craig argued. "You must remember a few good things about that time in your life."

"Some," she admitted. "But a lot of those memories are pretty rotten."

Craig countered with a sympathetic smile. "I know

the story, or one of them, at least. Your mother told me about your one and only attempt at calf roping. In fact, that's where I got the idea for this joint project of ours."

"Nothing's sacred anymore. And for your information, there was no rope involved," Dee retorted as she focused the camera and quickly snapped a shot.

Her accident hadn't occurred in front of a crowd of thousands, only her stepbrother and his friends. That had been humiliation enough for a fourteen-year-old girl who only wore a bra because her friends did. She'd been trying so hard to act grown up, to fit into a new home and a new lifestyle that seemed foreign and often unfriendly. Her childhood in the city hadn't prepared her for dealing with manure underfoot, cattle taller than herself, or the grim practicality of a working horse ranch, albeit a small one.

When she'd found the calf caught in the tangled barbed wire, she'd thought she could free it herself and finally prove herself useful. She'd nearly done it when the others had ridden up and startled the calf. It knocked Dee over and stepped on her in its frenzy to escape the horses thundering down on them.

Now she knew that none of the ensuing mess was her fault. At the time, though, the blood on her face and the six stitches had been the lesser of her wounds. Her stepbrother's laughter had hurt more. He had always seemed to be either laughing at her or yelling at her. He hadn't liked her much, no matter how hard she tried to make friends with him. He hadn't wanted a sister. Greater hurts and disappointments had followed through the years, but somehow the wounds of adolescence still cut deep.

Now, as she watched the eager faces of the youngsters lined up for the kids' calf roping, she thought more about the physical pain when the calf's hooves had kicked her arm and her forehead. The memory was enough to keep her on tenterhooks as she watched the swarm of rope-swinging youngsters pursue the scattering herd.

"Kids are tough," Craig reminded her after a particularly loud gasp.

"How would you know? You don't have any."

"You're forgetting I'm a teacher."

"Your students have children of their own."

"Lighten up. I started out with first-graders," he said, then raised his arm, pointing toward the arena gate. "Hey, the clowns are back. I wondered when we'd get another look at them."

Dee slapped his arm down. "Don't point. They'll take it as an invitation to pick on me again."

Craig chuckled. "I hope you got plenty of good shots of them. I wrote a whole chapter on rodeo clowns, so you'll need to do several illustrations."

"Just my luck," she retorted.

The cheers from the crowd in the bleachers turned her attention back to the kids in the arena. A lariat dropped over the head of a small, bald-faced Hereford, and a pair of dusty boys tugged the calf back to the judges. A tentative relief flooded through her as two other sets of contestants followed suit and the announcer called out the names of the winners. Then the rodeo clowns joined the fray and played the crowd for laughs while they persuaded the more persistent contestants to give up the fight.

"Tell me how it turns out," she said, handing her camera over to Craig. "This dust is raising hell with my contacts. I'm going to put some drops in my eyes. You want me to bring you a beer on my way back?" she asked as she stretched to her feet.

"Sure," Craig said, reaching for his wallet.

"No way," she replied with a wicked grin, waving

the money off. "I want to make sure you *really* owe me."

Still smiling, she worked her way through the crowd toward the brightly colored porta-potties stationed around the arena at strategic locations. Then she spotted one of the clowns and decided to talk to him for a minute. With all the dust, her shots probably weren't that good. Maybe she could talk him into a demonstration tomorrow, a sort of impromptu photo shoot, minus the bulls and the dust. It was the least he could do, considering how he'd embarrassed her.

Dee was about to cross the gravel drive to follow the clown when the clatter of hooves warned her to step back. Two cowboys on crowd-skittish horses trotted past, leaving a faint haze of dust in their wake. Squinting, Dee searched the other side for the clown, but he had disappeared.

She angled over to the gate and approached a gnarled cowboy in a battered, stained Stetson. His attention was focused somewhere to the left where one of the broncs was bumping against the board fence. She had to tap his arm twice before he turned and noticed her.

"Could you tell me where the clowns went?" Dee asked.

The man's bristly eyebrows arched, and he surveyed her from head to toe. "Maybe I could help you."

"I need to speak with them for a moment about a book I'm working on," she said, briskly erecting an invisible wall around herself with her cool tone and stiff bearing.

The man scratched his temple and studied her, as if trying to decide something. "Well, Matt's around someplace," he finally said. "The calf-ropin's about ta start. My guess is Nick's gone to change. You might try his trailer."

Dee nodded. "Where's that?"

"Oh, back there," he gestured with a wave of his arm. "A light-colored outfit hooked up to a beat-up black pickup. You can't miss it, parked back there under that dusk-to-dawn light. Can't see how the fools sleep with that thing shinin' all night."

"Thanks," Dee called as she hurried away.

She found the trailer with little trouble. The only thing the cowboy had neglected to mention was the loudspeaker that was also mounted on the light pole. Her first knock was smothered by a spit of static from the speaker, and she knocked again, louder this time.

"You lookin' for me or Nick?" a voice called from the back of a nearby pickup.

Dee glanced over as the clown with the strange hair jumped down and hoisted a saddle to his shoulder.

"You'll do." She introduced herself and explained her reason for seeking them out.

"I wish I could help you, especially since you were such a good sport out there. But you'll have to ask my partner," he said. "Right now, I have to talk to somebody and see if I can smooth over some ruffled feathers."

Dee frowned, preferring to avoid the clown who had humiliated her in front of two thousand people. "Where is your partner?" she finally asked.

"You just missed him," he said, stepping closer. "He should be back sometime in the next half hour or so, though, if you want to wait."

Dee withdrew a little further into herself at the gleam of interest in Matt's expression. "That's okay. I need to find someplace to rinse my eyes. I'd forgotten how much dust there is at a rodeo."

"Contacts?"

"Unfortunately," she replied, wishing she'd thought to wear her glasses instead, even if they did bump distractingly against the viewfinder every time she tried to take a picture.

"Use the trailer. Nick won't mind, and I know I don't." He flicked open the door, tapped a light switch, and peered inside. "Nope, nothing embarrassing lying around."

"Never mind, I think . . ."

"Look, Nick and I share this trailer when we're on the road. If I say it's okay, it's okay. Besides, there's nothing else around but porta-potties and cattle troughs, which probably aren't what you need," he said, backing away. "I've got to go now, but maybe I'll see you later."

After a moment, Dee shrugged and stepped inside, closing the door behind her. The place was a mess. A half-empty bowl of popcorn shared the table with various jars of paint. No, probably makeup, she corrected herself, remembering the line of work of the men who lived here. The built-in furnishings and appliances were worn, and a grocery sack stuffed with paper plates and styrofoam cups blocked the aisle. She stepped over it and landed on the hot-pink bra. Some hidden gadget in the garment squeaked, and Dee gaped in horror. She felt herself flush again and closed her eyes, thankful she was alone. Then her sense of humor overcame her sense of embarrassment, and she collapsed against the counter in a fit of giggles.

She picked up the watermelon-size bra, squeaked it again, and flung it over the back of an uncomfortable-looking chair. It took only a few seconds to locate the tiny bathroom and switch on the light. A makeup-stained towel was lying across a tiny sink. A bit of red came off on Dee's fingers when she tossed the towel aside. Peering in the mirror, she frowned at her red-rimmed, irritated eyes, then pulled the bottle of drops from her pocket.

Outside, the speaker on the pole roared the crowd's applause, then fuzzed with static, making the announcer's words unintelligible. She thought he said something about bronc riding and hoped this clown showed up soon. The bull riding scared her half to death, but she'd always liked to watch the broncs. The stubborn, half-wild horses that refused to be ridden somehow appealed to her. They were misfits, too, and she used to root for the horse instead of the rider. Fortunately, she'd had enough sense, even then, to keep that bit of sentiment to herself.

Blinking hard, she wiped away the moisture, then added more drops to her eyes. The speaker blared again, and she grinned at her blurred reflection in the mirror. She just might make it through the night, and even the next day. She was a grown woman, not an insecure adolescent. She didn't need to fit in here, and it didn't matter whether she was an outsider. Plus, she'd already experienced the worst that could happen. Everything was downhill from here.

THREE

"Tough luck tonight, missing that calf like that," the grizzled cowboy at the gate said, slapping Nick on the back when he passed through.

Nick nodded, said something, and handed the reins to the bulldogger from Austin. Disgusted with himself for letting a pair of gray-green eyes haunt him to the point of distraction, he headed back to the trailer. He had about half an hour yet to change into his clown clothes and smear his makeup back on.

Maybe he could manage that without screwing it up, he thought. Missing the calf couldn't be helped, not really. If he'd had his mind completely on the business at hand, he might have anticipated the animal's evasive move and caught him anyway.

But he couldn't forget that woman's eyes. Or that scar. It really *was* her. The day-dreaming girl had grown up quite a bit, he thought with a sneer. The white-haired man beside her wasn't her father. He wasn't a stranger, either, because she'd clutched his hand when Nick had climbed the fence.

An acrid, bitter taste filled his mouth. He paused, his hand on the trailer door. *She was beautiful.* And she was wasting that on a man older than her father. It just didn't figure.

He opened the door and frowned at the lights that were on. Trust Matt to forget to turn them off. They'd run the reserve batteries down again if they weren't a little more careful. Kicking the trash sack aside, he quickly shed his jeans and slipped on the over-size cut-off overalls he wore for bullfighting. He bent over double and reached for his knobby-soled sneakers when he heard a loud and decidedly feminine-sounding gasp behind him.

Nick froze and closed his eyes.

"Maybe I *should* lock the door," he said. "Freda, if you don't get out of here right now I'll . . ." The words trailed off when he saw the gleaming black hair and the shocked gray-green eyes of the woman standing three feet away from him.

"Oh, my goodness," she whispered in a choked voice as recognition dawned in her expression.

Nick felt like the bottom had dropped out of his stomach. He watched her eyes darken as she stared, stricken and vulnerable. In two seconds flat, the expression in those eyes changed from trapped surprise to spitting cat. Then the faint smile line at the corner of her lips clenched into bitten-back fury. He remembered then what the Williams women were like. Williams or whatever name they took, they were like lightning, beautiful from a distance, but destructive up close. He tried, but didn't quite succeed in tamping back the surge of heat rising in his blood.

Slowly, he sank back into a chair and surveyed her with what he hoped was a cool, distant expression.

"How's life treating you, Sis?" he asked.

For a moment, Dee could only stare. Nick Ramsey was the last person she'd expected to see here. The last she'd heard, he was hundreds of miles from Kansas.

"I'm not your damned sister," she ground out.

"Well, I'm not feeling especially brotherly right now. Exactly how long have you been hiding? And when did you come out?" he demanded.

Dee felt the blood rush to her face as she recalled the flash of red underwear that his pants had covered the instant she stepped out. "Never mind that. What are you doing here?"

"I think that's pretty obvious," he said, punctuating his answer with a brief laugh.

Dee glared. "I need to talk to the clown. Do you know when he'll be back?"

"Any second," Nick said. She noticed his lips twitched with suppressed amusement as he reached for a jar of red makeup and toyed with the lid. For the life of her, she couldn't figure out what was funny. She couldn't decide whether she was more embarrassed or angry about the situation she found herself in.

Dee bit her lip, wishing she could simply sink through the floor. Or better yet, make it to the door without having to squeeze past him. She couldn't believe what just happened, or that she'd reacted to the sight of him like a fifteen-year-old. But she'd been fifteen when Nick had left the farm. A month later, she and Pam had been gone, too. And she'd never considered the possibility of seeing him again.

"I'm sorry," she said. "I had no idea you were in here, or, well, I didn't hear the door. The other guy, the one with the weird wig, said I could wait in here and that his partner would be right back. But either he didn't know you were using this trailer or he played a really rotten joke." Now she was babbling. Fearing further regressions, she clamped her jaw shut.

That's when it hit her. He was in his sock feet, wearing all the trappings of the clown who had kissed her, all but the makeup. Except he still wore traces of that.

She could see a smudge of white at the hairline and a faint streak of red on the side of his nose. Red, like the smear on the bathroom towel. Red, like the grin of the clown who had kissed her.

"You knew who I was!" she accused. "You knew and you made me the butt of that stupid joke."

He at least had the grace to wince. "I didn't know until it was too late. Matt picked you out."

"What do you mean until it was too late? And since when are you working as a rodeo clown? Last I heard you were riding bulls and working on some ranch in Texas."

"That was ten years ago."

"I know it was. I haven't seen you since the divorce. It's been almost that long since I heard of you, not that it matters a flying fig."

He sat down at the table. "Ah, yes. The divorce. How is your mother these days? Married again? And you? I don't see any rings so I'd guess that . . . older man you're with isn't your husband."

Dee lifted her chin and closed her expression. "I'd like to leave," she said. "If you'll just move your feet out of the way. . . ."

"Why? Seems like we have a lot of catching up to do."

"I think not," Dee replied coolly. Not for a million dollars would she fill in the details of those ten years. Her mother's third marriage and subsequent divorce, Dee's own flighty attempt at domesticity—all the mistakes and regrets were best left undisturbed. Nor would he be interested in the good things that happened to them. He didn't care. He never had. Otherwise, he wouldn't have been so mean to her when they were supposed to be brother and sister. Only they hadn't been. Not really.

When he stared at her like this, she wanted to

squirm, to explain herself so he wouldn't misjudge her. Damn it, she was thinking like a fifteen-year-old again. She raised her eyes defiantly, telling herself she didn't care what he thought, not after all this time.

"Are you going to let me out or not?" she asked.

Nick didn't move. His eyes held hers, measuring and judging, until she had to look away. Tucking her hands into her pockets, she waited a moment, staring out the window into the starkly lit night. She saw only the imprint of his face on her mind, the flickering uncertainty in his expression. She thought she heard a whisper of movement. But when she glanced over, he was still watching her from the chair and his legs still blocked the aisle.

She shifted as she picked out the similarities between this older Nick and his father, her former stepfather. They both had the same short, curling hair that barely obeyed a comb, the slightly crooked incisor that marred what was otherwise a model-perfect pair of teeth. There were lines now at the corners of Nick's eyes, crinkles that hinted at the laughing, good nature he'd inherited from his father. The only difference was that Nick had always resented her. He'd gone out of his way sometimes to avoid her. Tony, on the other hand, had charmed her into liking him, no matter how much she'd tried not to in the beginning.

And that was the problem with Tony Ramsey, she remembered her mother explaining once. Tony had an almost boyishly handsome face and an easygoing, fun-loving nature that some women couldn't seem to resist. He didn't have to adjust or compromise, because there was always some other woman to take him on his terms. Who could live with that for long? Pamela Norton Williams Ramsey had tried, but life on Tony's terms was too great a stretch.

And there in Nick's eyes, was the laughing glint that

shone out so much like the Tony that Dee remembered. It was enough to bring her to her senses and raise the hair on the back of her neck.

"How is Tony?" she said softly when she finally got around to speaking. "Still tomcatting around?"

She'd intended to make Nick angry, but instead he seemed startled. "As much as he can," he said after a moment.

"I can't say I'm surprised," she commented, letting her hands drop to the side as she edged her way determinedly toward the door. She only hesitated an instant at his feet before stepping nimbly over them. Her hand was on the knob when he spoke.

"Wait." His fingers closed over her forearm. She could feel the heat of his body behind hers, and shivered with unexplainable awareness. "I'm sorry," he continued. "This is silly, us snapping at each other about something that happened a long time ago."

"You're right," she agreed. "Let's just pretend I didn't see you, in any sense of the word. And you didn't see me." Dee started to pull her arm away, but he tightened his grip, not enough to hurt, but enough to make her glance sharply at his face.

He studied with puzzled eyes that seemed to peel away the veneer of maturity to reveal the child she had been—still was to a certain small extent. When he inhaled slow and deep, a slumberous look came into his eyes. Dee's mouth went suddenly dry. She tried to swallow.

"Whatever happened to the nice kid who traded me riding lessons for sketches of my horse?" Nick asked in a near whisper. The loudspeaker outside the trailer blared again, but Dee barely noticed, she was so caught up in the Ramsey spell. Her mind recognized it, but the rest of her refused to listen to the warning.

She drew a deep, shaky breath when his voice

dropped lower still. "Where's the girl who stayed up all night with that sick colt?" he said, moving around her so that she was forced to look at some part of him. She chose the bottom of his chin.

"She grew up and found out that some things can't be saved. You were right. Sometimes it's stupid to try," Dee said huskily. She was touched in spite of herself that he chose to remember more than the razor-tongued brat she'd been those last months before her mother packed them both up and left for the city.

Inside, she felt a dangerous softening as her thoughts split into two paths. The one remembered the innocence and intensity of a teenage crush and felt the stirring of less innocent yearnings. The other noted with cynical accuracy how easy it was to allow old memories to dupe you into acting foolishly. Hadn't she gone back to David twice under similar misconceptions? Except she'd known David better, much better than this man, who had been a stranger for all of her adult life. And David had at least claimed to want her.

"Just let go of my arm," she said in a low, level voice that vibrated with the effect of her mixed emotions. His hand trailed away reluctantly as he stepped back.

"Why were you taking pictures?" he asked.

"Work," she said as she twisted the doorknob until she felt it release.

"What does that have to do with me?"

She stepped out of the trailer. "Nothing now that I know who you are," she said, then closed the door with as much restraint as she could manage. She half expected him to follow and angrily demand an explanation. Instead she heard a low chuckle from the other side of the door.

Something snapped inside her at the sound. He was laughing at her *again*. A wild fury flared, and she kicked the door hard. Pain jarred through her toes and up her leg as she grabbed her foot, cursing silently.

After hobbling a few steps, she leaned against the side of a pickup truck until the pain dulled, then flexed her toes a couple of times. Nothing seemed broken, and the ache was fading fast. "Stupid," she told herself. "Really stupid."

Then another thought occurred to her and she backtracked to look at the door. A size seven sneaker print marred the smooth metal finish. Beneath the print was a fresh dent.

Dee's hand covered her mouth before she spun away, her knees weakening with reaction to everything that had happened there. The speaker above her blared, then scratched and sputtered out, covering any further sound from inside the trailer. It didn't matter, though, because in her mind she could still hear him laughing.

She drew a deep breath and walked shakily toward the bleachers. She only looked back once. Then she told herself it was just her imagination that one of the blue curtains in the trailer window moved.

FOUR

By the time Dee reached her seat, the trembling in her limbs had stopped. She'd mulled the encounter over and come to the conclusion that she'd reacted out of shock. The stirring attraction she'd felt was nothing more than leftover memories, nostalgia if you will. It had nothing to do with the reality of here and now, or even the reality of those final weeks at the farm when the only words out of anyone's mouth were sharp-edged.

"Where's my beer?" Craig asked, his eyes on the chutes. He handed over her camera without ever turning around.

"The line was too long," she improvised quickly. She'd forgotten it entirely, but she wasn't about to explain why. She just wanted to put that encounter behind her. In fact, she'd like to put this entire weekend behind her and hightail it back home this minute. Unfortunately, Craig was intent on hanging around until the rodeo's end tomorrow night, and she couldn't think of a convincing excuse for leaving.

Dee stared out at the arena and gradually she began to focus on the details again. When the next ride was over, Craig turned his attention back to her.

"It all happens so fast, I don't know how you can even have time to focus the camera," he said, then paused as a frown deepened the lines on his forehead. "Are you okay?"

"Sure. Why?"

"You're pale. You look sick."

"Thanks, Pops. I'll call you next time I'm feeling blue and need a pick-me-up."

"Dee, you're white as a sheet."

She shrugged. "I ran into somebody I knew a long time ago. I guess it was a bit of a shock seeing him."

"Him? What happened?"

"It was no big deal," she insisted.

He lifted a skeptical brow, but a murmur of excitement from the crowd distracted him from any further questioning. Relieved, she took a deep breath and held it for an instant before releasing it. Already she was beginning to relax among the safeness of the crowd. Tomorrow she'd laugh about the entire mess, she told herself.

"You missed a good ride," he said. "The second bronc rider really was unbelievable. I hope you don't mind, but I took a few shots. Maybe one or two will turn out."

Dee hid a smile. She'd have some great shots of hoof action. Craig's photos were always in perfect focus. But his aim was off, and he tended to cut off the heads of his subjects.

The next few events passed in a pleasant blur, and she actually began to enjoy herself. Then Craig excused himself and headed for the announcer's booth to clear up a few questions that had occurred to him during the rodeo.

Shortly after, the final heat of the bull riding was announced, and the two clowns lumbered into the arena. Feeling the tension tighten her muscles, Dee braced herself for further humiliation and wished she'd gone with Craig. Nick, she figured, would be ready to pay her back for denting his door. To her surprise, he ignored her completely. The riders themselves put on a good show, and only once were the clowns called upon for rescue. When it was over, her hands ached from the fist-clenching tension. After that, the bleachers emptied as the crowd streamed toward the field that doubled this weekend as a parking lot.

She packed up her gear then flopped back down on the bench to wait for Craig. She kept expecting Nick to appear and demand recompense for the damage to his trailer. Or maybe she hadn't made the dent at all. Maybe it was already there, and her sneaker had only happened to land on top of it.

By the time Craig returned, her own thoughts had made her edgy. "Did you find out what you needed to know?" she asked as they fell into step behind a large family.

"Some," he said. "Did you know that there are about three hundred rodeo bullfighters in the Professional Rodeo Cowboy Association. Only about twenty-five actually make enough to live on."

"You're kidding?" she exclaimed with a sudden chill. *And which category did Nick fall into?*

"That's what the announcer told me. A few do quite well, though not many," he continued. "Come on, let's drop the camera at the motel and then get something to eat at that place across the street, Frank's, I think."

She frowned, thinking that Nick might show up there since it was so close to the rodeo arena. "Maybe I'll just turn in."

"Not a chance," Craig insisted. "You haven't eaten since this morning, and you're still looking pale."

His worried expression made her feel guilty for not

confiding the real reason for her pallor. "You win, Pops. I'll get something to eat with you," she said with more enthusiasm than she felt.

He ruffled her hair, then reverted to the gentleman by taking the heavy camera bag from her shoulder. "You're going to be lopsided," he commented.

"Better you than me," she sassed back, then diverted his attention to the book and the bits and pieces of information he still lacked.

It took them another twenty minutes to make their way back to the motel and drop off the camera at Dee's room. Then they made the requisite phone call to Pamela, who reminded Craig once again about Dee's cynical attitude toward cowboys and all things western in association.

"Sounds like the pot calling the kettle black," Dee told him a few minutes later as they crossed the highway to Frank's. "You should have heard her when I first told her about this book of yours. She warned me not to accept the commission for the illustrations. She said I couldn't be objective about cowboys. What does she think I'll do, paint them cross-eyed?"

"And knock-kneed," he responded with a shrug. "You know I had a phobia about accountants for a long time, thanks to my CPA ex-wife. It goes away, given enough exposure."

"It must. Either that or you're a glutton for punishment. Does Mom know?"

"Worry about yourself, not my love life," he retorted.

Dee smirked. "Touchy, aren't you? Well, don't worry. I don't have a phobia about cowboys, just a healthy sense of self-preservation."

"If that's the case, you'd better change the subject. Barroom brawling isn't my scene," he pointed out as he pulled open the door to Frank's.

The place was bigger than she had expected, with a dance floor in the middle and tables around the perimeter. Even so, it was packed with a combination of truck drivers, rodeo people, and Friday-night revelers.

Someone she didn't recognize waved wildly until she pointed Craig in that direction. When they reached the table, Craig introduced Dee to the announcer, a tall, well-built man with only a trace of a pouch above his belt. A well-tanned, dyed redhead named Susie-something hung on his arm.

"Glad to see you finally got here," the man shouted, shaking Craig's hand. Then he made the rounds of the long table, reeling off a string of names that Dee barely caught. When the band picked up a lively country tune, half the table emptied, leaving room for the newcomers.

Two minutes later, Craig was engrossed in a conversation about the unwritten rules of rodeo etiquette. Dee listened with interest while tapping her foot to the beat.

"What can I getcha? Drinks? Food? Chips?" the waitress asked. "We got roast beef or ham-and-cheese sandwiches."

She leaned over their table, piling a handful of empty glasses onto her tray while she acknowledged their orders with a brief nod.

"Beer and a ham sandwich," Craig said, then glanced at Dee, raising his brows with the question. "Chablis?"

She grinned and shook her head. "The same as the gentleman," she said aloud, then leaned over to whisper in his ear. "When in Rome . . ."

"Brat," he retorted, then turned back to the announcer. She leaned back in her chair and closed her eyes as the band slipped smoothly into a slow, sad song. She opened them again when her beer came. She sipped carefully, allowing her taste buds to accustom themselves to the flavor. She hadn't had beer since college, and even then, she'd never been overly fond of it. It didn't even start tasting good until the bottom of the first bottle, and drinking more than two was asking for trouble. She was halfway through the bottle and her fourth dance refusal when she noticed the chair across from her was no longer vacant.

"How's your foot, Sis? Or was it your fist that put that dent in my trailer door?"

Dee winced at the old nickname, spoken in the remembered mocking tone. Beside her, Craig shifted his chair in her direction.

"Dent?" Craig's tone conveyed his disbelief. "Did he say something about a dent?"

"Sorry. I'll cover any reasonable repair charges," she said, putting the emphasis on the word reasonable.

"You dented his trailer? With what?" Craig looked startled. Dee supposed he'd never seen her lose her temper. Come to think of it, she hadn't been that angry in years, not since she'd caught David in her bed with one of his models. It seemed odd, even to her, that she'd react so strongly to Nick's laughter.

"I think she kicked it. The dent's about so big," Nick said, holding his thumb and forefinger about three inches apart.

"Doesn't anybody care that I could have broken my toe?"

Nick chuckled. "You were walking just fine from what I could see."

She flushed at the obvious appreciation in his tone and looked away. *That explains the curtain moving.*

"Dee?" Craig prompted.

She shrugged, pretending a nonchalance she didn't feel. "It was a light door. Besides, I was really angry." She stared down into the bottle, then tipped it up and took a large swallow. It still tasted horrible, but the action gave her time to think.

"When was this? Is that what upset you, why you were so pale when you came back to the bleachers?" His voice held a suspicious note that grated on Dee's already irritated nerves.

"I don't want to talk about it. It's done and over with." She'd been afraid this would happen. And she couldn't for the life of her think of a way to explain this to Craig without delving into the past—which ought to stay buried. However, the look on his face warned her that he wasn't going to let her drop the subject.

She took another sip before she spoke. She needed fortification for this. "Craig, meet Nick Ramsey, the rodeo clown with the obnoxious smile. He's also my former stepbrother."

"Oh, Lord," Craig muttered under his breath. "Pam was right. This trip was a mistake."

"Pleased to meet you," Nick said, holding out his hand. She noticed, however, that his expression held a challenge, as if he expected to be snubbed. After an initial hesitation, Craig returned the greeting, albeit in a somewhat doubtful tone.

"You're a close friend of Dee's?" Nick continued.

"Of course. She didn't tell you?" Craig said.

Dee groaned aloud at the hint of a sneer in Nick's expression. It was obvious what conclusion he'd drawn. She opened her mouth to explain, then thought better of it. Let him think what he liked. What did it matter to her? But it did matter, she realized, and that thought disturbed her.

"Craig writes children's books," she said instead. "I've illustrated a couple, and now we're working on a rodeo book. That's why we're here. Craig, didn't you have a couple of questions about bullfighting?"

Craig's strange look warned her that she'd been babbling again, and she cursed Nick Ramsey silently for rattling her so much.

"If you want to know about bullfighting, you need to talk to the cowboy over there," he said, pointing toward a group by the pool table on the opposite end of the room. "The tough old guy with the big eyebrows. That's Pete Granger. He taught me most of what I know. I figured the rest out on my own while I was shinnying up the fence with a bull on my tail."

A spark of interest lit Craig's gaze as he picked out the grizzled cowboy, the one who had given her directions to Nick's trailer earlier. "That's Pete Granger, huh? I've heard of him. I think maybe I'll go over and introduce myself."

Dee knew a moment of panic as she watched Craig rise from his chair. "You'll be fine, won't you, Dee? Let me know when the sandwiches get here." When she didn't answer, he touched her hair. "Or I could stay here with you, if you'd rather."

"Good move. You don't want to face that temper of hers," Nick interjected.

"Go on," she ordered in a resigned tone. "I promise not to assault the man until after you've had a chance to ask your questions."

"Are you sure?" She was surprised at the depth of concern in his expression, which was almost fatherly—she didn't know how else to describe it. She didn't know whether to be disturbed or touched.

"I'll be fine," she said with what she hoped was nonchalant unconcern. "Really," she added when Craig looked doubtful. "Nick and I lived in the same house for three years without breaking the furniture over each other's heads. I think we can manage to be civil for a few minutes in a crowded room."

"It's not the furniture I'm worried about," Craig said.

"You should be," Nick said with a teasing smile.

Dee was tempted to kick him under the table, but

somehow she resisted. After another hesitation, Craig turned and meandered across the room.

Left alone with Nick, she considered ignoring him. But she figured that would be childish, as well as an exercise in futility if he was determined to get her attention. And he was.

"What you said about us living in the same house wasn't strictly true," he said.

"You were gone a lot," she replied. "It was still your room, your house."

"Didn't you ever wonder why I was gone so much?"

"Rodeos. Hauling cattle. Other jobs."

"And that's all?" He seemed relaxed, leaning on the table like that, but his eyes caught hers with an intensity that disturbed her.

"It's no secret that you didn't like me or Mom."

He shook his head. "That's not strictly true either. So why aren't you dancing?" he asked, neatly changing the subject.

Something, probably the toe of his boot, trailed up her calf, and she shifted sideways. He wasn't coming on to her, was he? Nick? Her stepbrother? *Ex-stepbrother.* His knee bumped hers under the table.

"You want the truth or my usual response to worn-out lines like that?"

"Still sharp-tongued, too," he commented.

Her only answer was a slight shrug as she scanned the crowd for Craig, who had momentarily stepped out of sight. "He's over by the pool tables," Nick supplied, earning himself another scowl. "As I remember, you used to go to the school dances. And I know for a fact that you didn't sit around watching everyone else."

She shrugged and took another sip of the warming beer. "I'm just not in the mood right now."

"Or maybe this isn't your kind of music. I know this isn't the symphony, but it's not bad stuff."

Dee straightened. He'd just called her a snob by implication, and she bristled with offense. "The music's fine. The company's fine, or it was until a minute ago," she said, turning deliberately away from him and downing the rest of her beer. This time, the grimace was unavoidable. "I wish I had that ham sandwich to wash this stuff down," she grumbled.

Noting the telltale twitch at the corner of Nick's lips, she deepened her frown and glared, daring him to laugh at her again.

"You hate beer," he commented.

"How perceptive of you," she said, rising from her chair and threading her way through the crowd toward Craig. Enough was enough, and the man's company was wearing on her nerves. As she walked, she rubbed the tense knot at the base of her neck and wished she'd brought some aspirin. When she reached the pool tables, she took his arm and squeezed lightly.

"Take a break, Pops, and let's dance. You'll still be here when we get back, won't you?" Dee addressed the last bit to the grizzled man who was eyeing her with recognition.

"I thought you weren't in the mood," Nick interjected from behind her. Startled that he'd followed her, she glanced over her shoulder.

"You changed my mind when you refused to go away," she said clearly. She could tell her jab hit the mark from the whoops and jeers behind her as she and Craig walked away. Hoping the men around the pool table would harass Nick unmercifully, she tugged Craig onto the dance floor and tried to remember the two-step.

On their second turn around the floor, she caught Nick's eyes on her, and she stumbled. Craig caught her before she could fall and truly humiliate herself.

"Are you upset about that Ramsey guy showing up?" he asked, then grunted as she trod on his toe.

"Sorry. No, not really." She hesitated. "Yes, maybe a little."

"Is that your final decision?"

"He always irritated me, that's all," she said. "He never liked me."

"He seems reasonable enough," Craig argued. "He had every right to be angry with you. Whatever made you kick his door?"

Dee grinned. "I lost my temper."

Craig missed a step. "This isn't an inherited trait, is it?"

"Yes, but don't worry about Mom throwing her calculator at you. I think the temper comes from my father. Besides, it takes a lot to set it off."

"I guess you didn't get along when you were all living on that farm or ranch or whatever it was," he said.

If only that was all there was to it. "He really wasn't around much then, so I guess we got along okay until our parents started fighting. Then we couldn't help but take sides."

Her eyes strayed back toward Nick, then darted away when he graced her with a slow, heated smile that barely turned the corners of his mouth but sparked fire in his eyes. Dee gulped, realizing then what a potent combination he was bringing to bear against her. She'd never thought curly, dishwater-blond hair and freckles could have such a devastating effect on her these days. Except for a brief crush on Nick when she was fourteen, she'd always been drawn to the tall, dark, handsome type—urbane men like David. He had understood her, even if he hadn't turned out to be the kind of man she could live with for the rest of her life. And Nick was none of these things. He was the all-American male, the guy next door, everyone's brother. Worse, he was too firmly grounded in reality, and he always had been.

"That's enough," Craig said with a wince, breaking into her thoughts. He whirled her around and pointed her back toward the table. "Go step on somebody else's feet. I'm too old for this."

"What? Did I do it again?"

"Hard," he asserted. "And you weigh a lot more than I thought."

Dee glanced over at the table again, then quickly away when Nick winked. "Maybe I'll check on those sandwiches," she said.

"Maybe we should just go back to the motel."

She gave his arm a squeeze. "Sorry. It's stupid to let him rattle me. You go on ahead and talk to the guys and find out what you need to know. I'll track down some food for us."

"Get me another beer, too, will you?" he said over his shoulder as he moved away. Dee glanced around, trying to determine how to track down their lost order. She was still standing there, scanning the room for the waitress when Nick touched her arm.

"Looking for a new partner?" he asked in a mocking tone.

"Looking for the waitress. Craig and I ordered sandwiches." As she spoke, she spotted the harried woman on the far side of the room, and she stepped in that direction. For the second time that night, Nick's fingers closed on her arm, stopping her.

"Go on and sit down and I'll take care of it. What did you order?"

"I'm a grown woman now. I can find myself a sandwich."

"You're still mad, aren't you?" It was more a statement than a question.

"Shouldn't I be?" she asked, louder than she realized until she noticed several people staring at them.

"Come on, we're attracting attention," Nick said, tugging her into the crowd of dancers and pulling her close. As luck would have it, the song was sad, the beat slow. "Let's settle this," he added. "Now. Quietly. Or we take it outside and shout it out."

"I don't have anything to say," she said, moving stiffly, the restless tension building in her to an unbearable pitch.

His hands at her waist burned her through the loose cotton blouse, and the touch of his knees against her leg sent tingling frissons from nerve to nerve. She wanted to be angry with him. It was illogical, this confusion of feelings his touch was evoking. It was unexpected. And frightening.

"You didn't used to stay mad for long. As I remember, you used to get fighting mad, yell a little, maybe throw something, then go off and cry about it. After that, it was pretty much over with, except for that one time." As he spoke, he lifted her bangs and touched the tiny half-moon scar on her forehead. "That one lasted a few days."

"That one hurt." She didn't mean physically, either, but he took it that way.

"You brought it on yourself. You should have gotten help."

"I know," she said, drawing back slightly from the hand that still rested in her hair. "I just thought I had to prove something. And when I failed, in front of you, God, and everybody, it hurt worse than I could imagine. And you guys laughed."

He kissed the scar, and this time she was too startled to move away.

"I didn't laugh," he whispered. He still clearly remembered every minute, every detail of that afternoon. He'd been terrified for her.

"Your friends did."

"They were jerks."

"It took you ten years to come to that conclusion?" Dee taunted, but in a soft, teasing tone that stirred the wanting that was growing within him.

"I'm just a dumb cowboy," he teased back, pulling her closer and inhaling sharply when he felt the light brush of her breasts against his chest.

"Never dumb, Nick. I never thought that," she said, her gaze softening. He knew by her light gasp when she felt his hardness against her hips. He let her pull back a bit, putting bare inches of space between them. He ought to pull away even more, leave the dance floor—leave this place altogether. Alone.

What did he know of her now, besides the fact that she had an exquisite body and soft hazel eyes? He hadn't seen her since she was fifteen. He didn't know what had happened to her since then or what she'd made of her life. Whatever it was, though, he had to find out, if only to satisfy the gnawing curiosity that had drawn him to her table.

She'd been untouchable then, his sister by marriage, but his sister nonetheless. And she'd been too young to understand why he'd pushed her away with his laughter and biting words so many times. He hadn't dared let her close, even then. Especially then. But she wasn't his sister anymore.

"Can we call a truce?" he whispered close to her ear.

"I'm not sure. The bra routine was a pretty low blow," she answered.

"I tried to stop him," he argued.

"Baloney. You dragged him off the fence and took over the gag yourself."

"Believe me," he said. "It was better that way."

"Why. What would he have done?

"You don't want to know."

"Tell me."

"Come to the rodeo tomorrow night. You'll see how he usually pulls it off."

Dee chuckled. "The bra or the stunt."

"Unfortunately both."

He felt the quiver in her shoulders as she laughed, a full, throaty sound that had deepened and matured from the girlish giggle he remembered. And something inside him turned over at the sound.

The music faded away, then flared up again in a twittering guitar solo. Then the other dancers exploded into a raucous, foot-stomping rendition of the Orange Blossom Special. "I think I'll sit this one out," she said, with a sheepish smile. "I practically flattened poor Craig's toes awhile ago."

He tried to suppress a grin and utterly failed. He knew, or at least he hoped, he'd been the cause of the distracted missteps he'd witnessed. Wary of stirring up her temper again, he wisely kept that knowledge to himself.

Once Dee was seated next to Craig, back at the table, Nick went in search of something cold to drink. Five minutes and three brief conversations later, he returned with two bottles. Taking a seat at the far end of the table, he caught Dee's eye and held up a sweat-frosted bottle of Coke. He held his breath as she hesitated, seeming to weigh the promise of a cold drink against any misgivings she might have about him. Then a slow, wide smile stole onto her lips, and a wave of desire hit him like heat from the highway on a hot August day.

She murmured something to Craig, then she circled the table and sat in the empty chair next to Nick. He let her take a long drink of the cola before asking the question uppermost in his mind. He watched her throat move when she swallowed, then stared down the neck of his own bottle before she could look his way and see how she was affecting him.

"Why were you waiting for me in my trailer?" he asked.

"I was looking for the clown. I had no idea it was you."

"Or you'd have been a hundred miles away," he finished for her.

She sighed. "I don't know. I wasn't too interested in coming to this rodeo—any rodeo for that matter."

"Craig talked you into it?"

She shrugged. "He showed me the rough draft of his book. It's good. I'd be a fool if I turned down this commission. Anyway, I spotted the clown, you, and decided to talk to you about a photo session tomorrow. Between the dust and the spotty lighting, I'm not sure I'll have any shots that I can work from. Daylight shots would be better."

He nodded slowly. "And Pete told you to talk to me?"

"Yep."

"Why photos? I figured you'd follow up on your talent, study art in college, and then do whatever it is that artists do for a living."

She took another long drink and studied his expression to see whether he was mocking her. When she saw he was serious, she set the bottle down. "This is what artists do for a living. My clients are advertising agencies, magazines, and in the last couple of years, Craig's publisher."

"Are you good?"

She smiled. "I like to think so. Anyway, the photos are just for me to work from after I get back home. Everything here moves too fast for me to sketch in the details, and I'm afraid my memory is too faulty to depend on,'' she explained as her short, neatly trimmed nails drummed on the tabletop. Was she as nervous as he was?

Nick drew a deep breath, then plunged in. ''So is Craig just an author you work with?''

Now it was her turn to stare down the neck of her bottle as she spoke. ''What if I told you he was something more, that he's a very important part of my life.''

''I wouldn't believe it. You're not in love with him.''

She glanced up, her lips curving with amusement. ''That's not what I said.''

She was teasing him, and he cursed himself for revealing too much. ''I heard you call him Pops,'' he said, relaxing in spite of his slip. ''Is he your stepfather now?''

Her expression grew more serious. ''He'd like to be.''

''And Pamela isn't interested,'' he concluded.

She lifted one of her brows in a cynical arch. ''Let's just say she's grown a bit skeptical about the theory of marital bliss. She hasn't had the best of luck.''

''What about you?'' he probed. ''Are you altar shy? I don't see any rings on your finger. And your name is still Williams.''

Her glance dropped to the table, then back to his face. ''Are you so sure of that?''

''That's the name you gave Matt,'' he said, enjoying the teasing game she was playing.

''I kept my name when I got married,'' Dee said.

FIVE

The smile froze on Nick's face, then his jaw slackened with shock. He stared at her with startled eyes. "And?" he prompted.

"And what?"

He started to speak, then clamped his jaw shut and opened it again. "You'd damn well better tell me there's more, because I really don't like what I'm thinking right now. You're married?" The sharp edge to his tone warned Dee that he was inches from exploding.

Puzzled by his sudden change, she stared. "What are you talking about? Oh—" As the realization dawned, she grimaced. "I'm not sure whether to laugh or slap you. No. I'm not married, not anymore."

He dropped an arm over her shoulder and leaned close. "Then you'd better be a little more specific," he said. "Finish what you start."

She stiffened. She'd left him dangling with that comment about being married, but she got the distinct impression that he meant more than that. Was this a heavy-handed come-on or a veiled hint of advice she was too obtuse to understand?

Deciding not to take any chances, she leaned forward

and removed his arm. "Maybe you'd better take your own advice and explain just what it is that I should finish."

"I guess it wasn't much of a marriage if you didn't even take his name. I'll bet you had separate checking accounts, too." He looked faintly disgusted, which didn't surprise Dee in the least. She'd be a fool to expect Nick to understand how she'd ended up sharing a warehouse loft with a promising and passionate young sculptor.

She smiled and took a drink. "Sorry to disappoint you. I kept my own name for professional reasons," she said after the cool fizz of the cola had washed away some of the uncomfortable dryness in her throat. "So tell me how you came to be a rodeo clown?"

"What went wrong with your marriage?"

"I'm trying to subtly change the subject."

"Subtle as a nail in the foot. Never mind, though. It's none of my business anyway."

She shrugged. "It's not. But since you're so curious, I'll tell you. I made a mistake, and I fixed it the best I could." End of discussion.

"Did you love him?"

So much for none of his business, she thought. "What do you think?" She met his gaze head-on, wondering what was going on inside his head. Why was he so persistent?

He leaned closer, studying her expression. He knew she was hiding something, but he doubted she'd tell him what or why. The innocence he remembered was gone. In its place Nick sensed a cynicism that saddened him. Considering her parents' history, he expected her to be wary of marriage, of any promise of permanency. But there was something else in her eyes, a faint vulnerability that showed through the wariness.

"I think you thought you loved him, and that he

disappointed you somehow. And I'd bet you've been very careful since then,'' he finally said.

She looked away, thinking he saw too much. The Nick she'd known years ago had been kind at times. But this perceptiveness was new. Or maybe she'd just been too self-centered and immature to notice it before. It embarrassed her, the idea that he could have read her so easily and sensed the adolescent hero worship she'd felt before the calf incident. Could he now sense the attraction she felt as they sat together, their thighs barely touching? She hoped not, and moved her leg, as if that would put a halt to these crazy thoughts. He accepted her changed position with no more than an amused lift of his brow.

''Oh, good,'' she said, glancing up. ''The sandwiches, finally.'' She watched as the waitress set paper plates on the table in front of her and Craig. None of the others, she noticed, had ordered any food. Maybe they had been forewarned about the service.

She didn't much care at that moment. Her stomach reacted to the aroma of the food with a loud rumble. And for once she was grateful for the cover noise of the band. She lifted one triangular half of the sandwich and took a healthy-sized bite.

Mustard.

She dropped the sandwich back onto the plate and grimaced.

''What's wrong?'' Nick asked.

She lifted the top piece of bread. ''The yellow plague,'' she said, eliciting a deep, rumbling laugh from him.

''Mustard,'' he confirmed, examining the sandwich more closely. ''Sorry. I had one of those for lunch. I should have warned you.''

She shoved the plate away from her. ''Want this one?''

"Send it back," he suggested. "They'll make you another one."

"When? Next week?"

"You may have a point," he said, pushing his chair back. "Come on. Let's go someplace else. I know where I can get you a mean chili dog."

Dee cooled perceptibly at the hint of anticipation mixed with the warmth in his expression. She recognized the ploy, the let's-go-back-to-my-place-and-talk routine. She should have expected it. He was a man like any other, after all, and Tony Ramsey's son to boot.

"Don't worry about it," she said. "I think there's some potato chips in the car, maybe some fruit left over from the drive down here."

He took her chair, pulling it back from the table with her in it. His breath tickled her face as he whispered in her ear. "I heard your stomach. Potato chips won't tame that monster."

"Too bad," she said, glancing at her watch. "It's after midnight. No place else will be open, unless there's another bar and grill in town." Somehow, she didn't think a town this size could support two. Just the thought of another grease-stained paper plate, not to mention the mustard, brought on another grimace.

"It's not a bar. And I guarantee it's open. The food isn't great, but you can put your own condiments on, I promise."

Her spine stiffened a bit more. She was not going back to his trailer with him. In the first place, she resented his assumption that she would. In the second, she didn't even like the idea of being alone with him, not when electricity sparked wherever he touched her. The chili dog might be tempting, all grease notwithstanding, but she had no intention of getting herself into a situation she couldn't handle.

"I don't think so," she said, voicing her line of thought aloud in a tone designed to freeze icicles on the beard of any man within hearing distance. "I may have been foolish a time or two in my life, but I'm not stupid, Nick Ramsey."

He released his hold on her chair and settled back into his. "I wasn't making a pass at you, but apparently the idea has crossed your mind. I wonder why?"

"Probably because I've heard it all before," she replied, hiding behind a false facade of cool cynicism.

He eyed her consideringly. "Maybe I should have explained. I was talking about the Jiffy Stop. It's a couple of blocks over."

"Oh." Dee searched his face for any sign of subterfuge, and found only honest amusement.

"They have a selection of the usual junk food."

She felt a slow, sheepish smile creep onto her face. "Sorry. I guess I just assumed . . ." Her voice trailed off as she considered what she'd assumed. She should have known better anyway. "Well, you have been a bit pushy tonight," she defended.

His lips finally curved back into a smile. "I was curious."

"About me? I can't think why you'd be curious about anyone you used to call Chicken Neck," she said, rising from her seat and brushing past him. She cast a laughing, rueful glance over her shoulder as she walked away from him.

A moment later, she was back at his side. "I told Craig not to wait for me. Come on. The chili dogs are on me," she shouted over the music. When he nodded, she grabbed his hand and tugged him out of his seat.

Outside, the night seemed quiet compared with the combined music from the band and din from the crowd. In the distance, Dee could hear the faint hum of cars on the main drag through town and the closer sounds of a yowling tomcat and a car door slamming.

"So where's this Jiffy Stop?" she asked as they strode through the parking lot.

"About two blocks that way." He gestured in the general direction of the main street. Instead of looking where he pointed, her eyes were drawn to his hand and the skinned, bruised knuckles that had struck a bull on the flank hard enough to turn its attention away from its discarded rider.

Yet when he put that same hand to the small of her back, his touch was gentle. She felt a shiver that had nothing to do with the cooling temperature or the light breeze that had sprung up from the west.

"You don't mind walking, do you?" he asked. "My truck's still at the rodeo grounds."

"You said it was only a few blocks," she replied. She stooped to pick up a discarded beer can, using it as an excuse to move away from his disturbing touch. She tossed the can in a neat arc toward the barrel positioned strategically near the parking lot exit. When it clattered against the side and back onto the pavement, Nick chuckled and reached for it.

Dee eyed his rear end, thinking it presented a tempting target, one she wouldn't have hesitated to aim for ten years ago. With a slight giggle, she stepped forward and raised her foot, aiming it at the can instead. She kicked it out of his reach just as his fingers stretched toward it.

"Not bad for a girl," he murmured, then trotted past her to kick it across the street. The words echoed in her head as she remembered other times he'd said that. And for the first time, the memories were warm and happy, with no taint of bitterness. It was as close as he'd ever come to a compliment.

Laughing and taunting each other, they continued the

game down the length of the next two blocks until a patrol car rounded the corner and cruised slowly past.

"We'd better stop before someone reports us for vagrancy," she said. She snatched up the can from the curb and carried it the remaining block. "You never did answer my question earlier. How did you get started bullfighting?"

"I wasn't having much luck staying on them, but I found out I was pretty good at getting away," he said.

Dee glanced sideways, studying his expression in the stark light of a streetlamp. "Somehow I think there's more to it than that," she said.

"Not really," he said with a shrug. "That's pretty much how it happened. I suppose there are other things I could do. But I like rodeo, and I'm lucky enough to be able to make a living at it. Most cowboys consider themselves lucky if they make travel expenses."

"But you're not bragging," she commented, with a light jab to his arm. Then she let her hand drop self-consciously. He wasn't Craig or any one of her other friends. Fortunately, he didn't seem to place any significance on her lapse into easy familiarity.

His self-effacing grin turned to a hearty peal of laughter. "No, ma'am. I'm not one to brag."

Taking the can from her hand, he dropped it into a trash barrel as they passed the gas pumps and headed for the door of the Jiffy Stop. Although it was after midnight, the place was still busy, probably thanks to the rodeo.

"Choose your poison," Nick said as he stopped in front of the freezers.

Dee strolled on past. "I believe you mentioned chili dogs," she said, stopping before the rotating warmer.

Helping herself, she assembled the various parts, then wrapped her chili dog in a napkin. "Still hungry?" she asked, noticing he'd come up behind her.

"I could eat one."

"Here," she said, handing over the chili dog she'd just made and fixing herself another. There was a brief tussle at the checkout counter over who would pay until Dee gave in. "Forgive me for insulting your male pride," she whispered as she left him there and sauntered out the front door.

She was sitting at the curb around the side of the building when he came out. "What was that crack supposed to mean?" he asked as he eased himself down beside her, only inches from touching her.

She licked a bit of chili from her lip, then wiped her chin. "I think I need a bib," she said, glancing up. The hot look in his eyes chased any other thoughts from her mind and at the same time torched a slow heat that fanned out from her midsection. He seemed fascinated with her mouth, and she hastily wiped her lips again with the napkin.

"You said something about insulting me?" he prompted.

That wasn't quite how she'd put it, but she wasn't about to point that out just now. "Chivalry," she explained. "Or chauvinism. One or the other is usually at work when a man insists on paying for food. He either feels threatened or he thinks he's buying more than the food," she finished in a cynical tone.

"That's the way I was raised," he said with a shrug. "I guess that's why we never had any money when I was a kid."

The hand holding Dee's chili dog stopped halfway to her mouth. Then she caught the dancing glints of laughter in Nick's chocolate-brown eyes. "Your dad never had any cash because he was always buying food for his lady friends?" she questioned, hoping she'd caught his drift.

"Something like that. I know. Weak joke."

She shook her head. "I'm just not used to joking about stuff like that."

"Sometimes it's easier to joke about serious things than to deal with them head-on. It takes some of the sting out of your problems."

She considered for a moment. "Maybe. And sometimes it's just another way of avoiding the issue."

She felt Nick's eyes on her as she took another bite, but when she glanced over a moment later, he was concentrating on his food. He finished before her, rolling the napkin and foil wrapper into a ball.

"So . . ." she began, as she wiped the last of the grease and chili drips from her hands a moment later. "In the last ten years you've learned to distract bulls and laugh at some of the little nasties life throws your way. What else have you been up to? Wives? Kids?" She asked the question lightly, but the answer was important to her. She'd surprised herself by liking him, by tingling where he touched, where he so much as looked. She didn't want to think she was drawn to what belonged to another woman.

"Almost," he said, adjusting his hat. Her question seemed to make him uneasy, and she felt herself stiffen.

"Almost what? Married or a father."

"As far as I know, there aren't any little Ramseys running around or even on the way. No, I mean I almost got married once."

"What stopped you?"

"Well," he drawled out. "Lack of a bride, for one thing. She changed her mind and eloped with Jack Miller."

"Jack Miller from down the road?" Dee practically squealed in her surprise. "She left you for that egomaniac? What an idiot!" Then she covered her mouth, hoping she hadn't stomped on any fresh wounds. "When did this happen?"

"Seven years ago. And don't feel too sorry for me. She ran off six months later with a feed broker."

She rolled her eyes. "Where did you find this woman?"

"You might remember her. Mandy Millikan."

Dee furrowed her brow, concentrating on the name. Then the picture sprang to mind of a cute little blonde with voluptuous curves tucked into a tight pair of Levi's and a fitted western shirt.

"I see you remember her," he said.

"Yeah. She taught me how to put on lipstick and eye shadow when we were at the rodeo in Bowling Green, Missouri."

"I remember that," he said. "You looked like a fourteen-year-old—" he began, then hesitated.

"Tramp is the word Mom used."

"That wasn't what I was going to say." He touched her hair, feathering the silken strands through his fingers. "You looked like a kid who couldn't wait to grow up, like you believed that would be the answer to everything that bothered you."

She felt the laughter fade from her, to be replaced by something much stronger and more complicated. He came closer to the truth than she would have believed anyone could. She began to think he'd understood much more than she'd given him credit for back then.

"I guess all kids think that," she replied. "Didn't you?"

He shrugged. "It was different for me. I always had the farm to come home to. I always had Tony. He has a lot of faults, but he's a great father."

Dee was silent. She supposed that from Nick's perspective, Tony was a good father. She just wasn't prepared yet to think of the man as good for anything. "It's late. Or early, close to one o'clock," she corrected herself as she glanced at her watch.

"Come on," he said, holding out his hand. "I'll walk you back."

She let him pull her to her feet. "You don't need to. It's the long way around to the rodeo grounds."

He raised a brow. "You really don't think I'm going to let you walk back alone, do you?"

"Yes?" she suggested hopefully. The vague possibility of arm-wrestling outside her door made her uneasy. She'd only begun to think of him in friendly terms, and she didn't want anything to spoil that.

"Not a chance, lady." His expression brooked no argument. Dee knew better than to even try. He'd always been stubborn about certain things, and ten years would only have taught him more methods for getting his own way. Instead, she reached up and tipped his hat from his head, catching it neatly in one hand.

"Only if you let me wear your hat," she teased, slipping it onto her head. It was too large, but when she stuffed her hair up into the brim, it fit better.

On the way back, they walked close, talking quietly so as not to disturb the people sleeping inside the houses they passed. They reached Dee's motel room door just as Nick finished telling about a prank of Matt's that had gone wrong.

Traces of light shone through the curtain of the room next to Dee's, and she chuckled. "Craig's waiting up for me."

Nick shook his head. "The guy acts like he's your father already."

Dee wrinkled her nose. "Mom's dragging her feet, but she'll come around. Craig's a lot better suited to her than—"

"Tony," Nick interrupted. "It's okay to say it. We both know it's true."

"Tony, or Dad, or even Milt."

"Milt?" Nick looked appalled. "He sounds like an aging country western singer."

Dee shook her head. "Don't even get me started on Milt. Fortunately, Dad talked some sense into her before she married the man."

Nick shook his head ruefully. "Tony thought that Pam and your father would get back together someday. I know they used to talk a lot when he came to pick you up for visits. I guess that isn't going to happen if Craig's so much in the picture now, huh?"

She studied his expression carefully. A couple of hours ago, she would have considered the comment nosy or snipish. Now she knew better. But there was one thing Nick didn't know.

"Dad died two years ago," she said softly, with the hint of sadness that still haunted her once in a while when she thought of losing him.

Nick touched her cheek. "Dee, I didn't know. Tony didn't, either, or he would have told me. I'm sorry. I know your father meant the world to you."

She smirked. "Daddy's spoiled little girl, you used to say. And you were right."

"It didn't hurt you any. I think I like the way you turned out."

Dee felt herself flush at the rare compliment. "I guess I was happier with him than with anyone else back then. Later on, I realized that I was happy because I could be myself with him. He was the only one who really understood me. He took me seriously." She struggled against the lump forming in her throat.

"Anyway," she continued. "You need to get back and get some sleep so you'll be ready for the rodeo tomorrow."

"You'll be there?"

"With my camera," she replied. "Which reminds me. Are you up to a photo session in the morning?"

"Just don't make it too early," he said, lifting his hat from her head. As her thick dark hair tumbled loosely around her shoulders, he stared hard, then reached out to touch it once again.

For a moment, she thought he was going to kiss her, and her heart beat crazily. Then he inhaled and backed away. He'd turned to leave when she spoke again.

"Nick?"

He spun back around and stared with an odd expression on his face. "Yes?"

"I'm glad we met again," she said.

He stepped slowly closer. "Me, too." His lips dropped to hers, brushing lightly in a soft caress that was as tender as it was brief. "Very glad," he said as he backed away, then disappeared around the corner.

SIX

Nick found it impossible to sleep as long as his late night warranted. Even if his body hadn't been attuned to waking at morning light, the slamming truck doors and drifting voices would have disturbed him. He dozed fitfully for a while, then the soft click of the trailer door brought him to awareness.

As his eyes focused, he noted the twisted sheet on Matt's empty bunk. Blinking hard, he stretched out as far as he could in the cramped bed tucked into the gooseneck of the trailer.

Last night had been full of surprises. The nicest had been the laughing glints in Dee's beautiful gray eyes once she stopped spitting like an offended kitten.

Chicken Neck. Nick stared at the mottled shadows on the ceiling above his bunk and groaned aloud. Trust Dee to remember what he'd called her when she was still in that awkward, gangly stage and afterward still when her teenage body had softened into interesting curves and dips. He wondered if she'd ever figured out that his teasing covered a growing affection for the black-haired imp she'd been then. None of those names fit now, he thought as he mentally traced the graceful curve of her neck down to the fullness beneath the blouse she'd worn last night.

He'd tried to treat her like a sister from the beginning when his father married Dee's mother. In time, Nick had discovered that what he felt wasn't brotherly love. It was deeper and sweeter, and altogether wrong. She'd been half child, growing into a woman. As she grew, it had become more and more difficult to be just her big brother. In his frustration, he'd lashed out at her, confusing and hurting her until he'd convinced her he didn't like her. He'd pushed her away to keep himself from overstepping the invisible bounds Dad and Pam's marriage had placed between the two of them.

Invisible lines and rules that didn't apply anymore.

Nick bounded out of his bed, not wanting to dwell on that thought. He grunted at the ache that shot through his left leg when he hit the floor. Flexing his ankle, he moved around the narrow space, alternately stretching and testing his weight on the sore limb while his mind dwelt on Dee.

What might have been didn't matter now. He hadn't been allowed to watch his Dee mature into womanhood. He hadn't been the first to kiss her or to teach her what love could be. She wasn't his Dee anymore—she hadn't ever been, really. Glad as he was that they'd met again, he was sorry, too. His sweet dream had clay feet, just like everything else in this world. She had a temper, an ex-husband, and a home in the city.

He told himself it was for the best. He'd been saved from making a major mistake. He was too much like Tony. And she was too much like Pam, all city polish and too world-wise to settle for farm life.

Nevertheless, he felt a hum of anticipation as he pulled on a fresh pair of jeans. Then, remembering the reason for the promised photo shoot, he changed his mind and took them off again. He'd just put on his clown gear and was starting on the makeup when Matt tapped on the window.

"You decent?"

Nick lifted the shade and grinned. "Is she here?"

"Hell, no. She took off last night before I had a chance to talk to her." Matt's face disappeared from sight for a moment as he opened the door and came inside.

Nick dropped the shade and turned back to the mirror. "Tough luck, friend. She'll be around today, but you can keep your hands to yourself. You're already in enough trouble as it is."

"What are you talking about? She left right after the barrel races last night."

Nick paused, a red-smeared finger halfway to his chin. "Oh, you're talking about Freda."

His partner cast a disgruntled look in Nick's direction. "Who'd you think I was talking about? And what are you doing anyway? I thought you and Pete were going out to look at that colt."

"Later," Nick interjected. "So Freda's still mad, huh?"

"I guess. She left this on the windshield of my truck." Matt delved into his pocket and pulled out a crumpled sheet of paper.

"What's it say?"

"Eat dirt. And that was the nice part."

Nick winced in mock sympathy. "I guess this means I won't be best man for a while." The only reply was a dirty towel flung in his face. Further attempts at conversation met with little more than grunts from Matt, so he soon gave up trying.

While Nick smeared white greasepaint around his eyes, his thoughts turned back toward the black-haired woman he was waiting for. They hadn't set a time, but she'd always been an early riser. He wanted to be ready when she got there, warmed up and loose with the stiffness worked out of his bad ankle.

It wasn't until Matt tapped him on the shoulder that Nick realized he was whistling. His last note went flat, trailing off into nothingness.

"You're feeling chipper this morning," Matt commented. "That wouldn't have anything to do with your late night or that lady you left Frank's with, now would it?"

Nick paused, biting back a retort. Word got around quickly. He should have considered that last night, but he'd been too intent on getting Dee out of the crowded, noisy bar to think of the effect on the rumor mills.

"I'm surprised you didn't recognize her. You met my stepsister a time or two, didn't you? She and her mother went along with me and Dad to a couple of rodeos," he explained in what he hoped was a nonchalant tone.

"You don't even have a grandmother as far as I can remember. How'd you get a sister?"

Nick released a low, short laugh. "Think way back. Dad's second wife. The one with the Porsche and the black-haired kid."

Matt's brows arched upwards. "Her? You mean you spent the night with her? The daughter of that cobra who cleaned out Tony? Are you nuts?"

"I spent the night here, or what was left of it."

"That's not what I heard."

Nick sighed. "Forget what you heard. Besides, you were passed out in your bed when I came in. You wouldn't have known the difference." It took only a moment to set his friend straight on a few other facts. When he finished, Matt was chewing his lip thoughtfully.

"So you're just helping this woman, your *former* sister, and the old man with the book?"

"Right."

"Must be a good feeling if it makes you whistle in the morning. Maybe you'll let me in on the secret. I feel like a dead horsefly. Freda's spitting mad and I didn't do anything to deserve it this time."

"She'll be in Oklahoma City next week. Maybe she'll cool down enough to listen to you then."

"Yeah. And pigs fly." Matt shrugged, but his heartsick expression indicated how upset he really was. Nick stared at his plate. It was none of his business. The worst thing he could do was make it his. He'd lose his two best friends if he interfered.

"Women," he muttered in a commiserating tone, then heaved an involuntary sigh of relief when Pete's gray head appeared at the window.

"You 'bout ready, Nick? Good grief, what're you up to? You're not going like that, are you?" The older man looked faintly uncomfortable at the prospect.

Nick glanced at the clock on the wall. Ten after nine, late by Pete's standards, and by his own as well. "Something's come up," he said. "You go on without me. If you think the colt's as good as that Harrington fellow says, let me know. I can look him over this afternoon or tomorrow."

Pete shrugged. "Whatever you say. Matt, you wanta come along and see if this little nag is worth the money that farmer is asking?"

Matt glanced glumly between the two of them. "Sure," he said. "It beats watching the traffic on Main Street." He grabbed his hat and followed Pete outside.

Nick puttered about in the trailer, tidying up and disposing of the accumulated trash. That finished, he settled down to leaf through the latest issue of the *Quarter Horse Journal* while he waited. Two articles and three trips to the window later, he set the magazine aside and glared at the clock. It was 10:45 and she still wasn't here. Surely she hadn't forgotten.

Tired of waiting, Nick grabbed his hat and headed for the arena. Maybe he'd misunderstood. Maybe she was waiting for him there. Or maybe she'd had second thoughts. He shouldn't have kissed her. But she'd said she was glad they'd met again. Had she lied?

Telling himself he was thinking like a fool, he scanned the rodeo grounds for her slight figure and shiny black hair. But he didn't see her, and neither had anyone else. By the time Matt and Pete returned, Nick didn't know whether he was angry or worried. Whichever the case was, he found it difficult to concentrate on Pete's assessment of the horse. After a brief consultation with the two men, Nick headed back to the trailer and removed the clown makeup. Then he climbed into his truck and headed for the motel.

Dee was still asleep when the thumping began. She rolled over and pulled the pillow over her head, and after a bit the thumping ceased. She had just drifted back into a pleasant dream when the phone jangled close to her ear.

She tried to ignore that, too, but whoever was calling refused to stop. Squinting against the sunlight that filtered through a crack in the curtains, she reached for the receiver and muttered into it.

"Craig? Is that you?"

"Rise and shine, you lazy bum. It's almost noon."

"Noon? *Noon.*" She bolted upright and flung the covers aside. "Why didn't you wake me up sooner. I had plans for this morning." A yawn caught her unprepared, and she nearly missed what he said next.

"Well, your plans came beating on the door," Craig's reply creaked over the line.

"What?" She rubbed at her sleep-blurred eyes and wondered whether she'd heard him right. "Craig, I just woke up. You'll have to be a bit more specific if you expect me to make sense of that."

"Nick's here."

"Oh!"

"When you didn't answer your door, he tried mine."

She twisted the phone cord, wide-awake and impatient now that she knew what was going on. "Tell him I'll be over in a few minutes. Just give me time for a quick shower." She hung up the receiver before Craig could reply.

Fifteen minutes later, she stepped outside into the heat wearing fresh jeans and a pink tank top. She'd flung a light cotton shirt in her bag for protection against the sun and piled her hair high atop her head in a neat knot.

Craig answered her light knock with a casual "Come in," and the door swung wide as he unlatched it and stepped away. The first thing she saw when she entered the room was Nick, lounging on the bed with his stained sneakers hanging off the edge. His grin widened as she flopped the camera bag down beside him.

"It's about time, lazy bones," he commented. "For a while there, I thought you'd either forgotten or left town."

Dee couldn't help the grin that stole onto her lips. "Now you know what a morning person I'm not," she replied, then immediately regretted it when she saw the subtle change in Nick's expression.

"I'll keep that in mind," he whispered, barely loud enough for her to hear.

She felt herself flush and turned away, nonplussed.

"What time did you get in, anyway?" Craig asked, seeming oblivious to the undercurrents. "I waited up figuring you'd want to talk or have a nightcap."

"You mean you wanted to give me a whole new list of instructions for the illustrations. You didn't want me for this job because I'm good. You wanted me because I'm the only artist you can browbeat into doing it your way."

"Well, I did have a few suggestions," he admitted. "I've been talking them over with your . . . with Nick. Exactly what are you two, anyway? I know what you said, but you'll excuse me if I'm confused."

Dee pursed her lips and glanced over at Nick. "Darned if I know, either," he said. "I take it neither of you have eaten yet?"

Craig grimaced. "Let me wake up first. I'm getting too old for this kind of life. I should be settled in a little house in the country with grandchildren at my feet every Sunday."

Dee emitted an indelicate snort. "Right. And I'm a purple anteater. Come on, Nick. Let's go find some food." She lifted the bag to her shoulder and started toward the door.

"That about sums it up for you," Nick said, slowly easing himself to his feet. "She barks and I feed her. It's always been that way."

"And well it should," she retorted. "See you later, Craig. Should we meet back here before dinner?"

"If I don't run into you sooner," he replied, then closed the door behind them.

Dee turned toward the street, but Nick caught her arm. "The truck's over here."

"Sorry. I figured we were walking."

Nick stopped beside the battered black pickup and opened the door for her. Before she could climb in, though, she felt his fingers in her hair.

"One more thing," he said as he plucked out the hairpin that anchored the knot of hair atop her head.

"What did you do that for?" she retorted, snatching at the pin until he tucked it into his jeans pocket.

"I like it better down."

"It's hot. And I can't work with hair in my face." When he refused to turn over the pin, she fumbled in the camera bag for a spare, but only found a thin, terry-cloth headband. Ignoring him, she pulled her hair back into a ponytail and twisted the band around it to anchor it. By the time she'd finished, he was sitting behind the wheel.

"Satisfied?" he asked as she climbed in.

Dee didn't answer. She felt foolish for making an issue of it, but his attitude irritated her. "Just what was all that about?" she asked, genuinely puzzled by his behavior. For a moment there, he'd acted like a possessive lover from a Grade-B movie. What was it with men and their hang-ups about women's hair? And why couldn't they answer a simple question, she added silently as he crunched the gears and drove out of the parking lot.

They were a couple of blocks from the Jiffy Stop when he finally answered. "I barely recognized you with your hair all tied up. You looked like somebody else, all cold and untouchable and completely in control of everything around you. That woman didn't belong here."

Dee released a sigh of irritation that feathered out her bangs. Just like old times. She didn't belong here. "So what else is new. I never did."

"You really haven't changed," he said. "You listen but you don't hear what I'm saying."

"And what are you saying? I'm a little obtuse before breakfast so you'll have to spell it out."

He started to speak, then braked the truck and turned sharply into the Jiffy Stop drive. As the truck rolled to a stop next to the building, he glanced over at Dee. "Well?" she prompted.

Nick switched off the engine and leaned on the steering wheel for a minute, staring straight ahead. Finally, he drew a deep breath and faced her, his expression set in an uncertain frown. "You looked like somebody's secretary, all proper and businesslike. Or one of those lady lawyers you see on TV. I started to wonder whether last night really happened or whether I dreamed it. I wanted the lady from last night back," he explained in a wistful tone.

"You conjured up all this from a hairdo?" she asked skeptically. What would he have done if she'd worn the silk harem pants? *Never mind*, she told herself quickly, not wanting to follow that line of thought any further.

He captured her hand and gave a gentle squeeze. "Come on," he said. "Let's see if they have any chili dogs left."

Dee chuckled, but inside she felt something catch in her chest with an almost physical pain. The feeling was so unexpected, it nearly stole her breath. Silently, she followed him to the frozen foods case. After a moment, the ache eased enough for her to speak normally when he asked her what she wanted.

"Don't they have any fruit here?" She walked on past, scanning the aisles until she located a refrigerator case near the cashier's counter. "There," she pointed triumphantly, then ordered two apples and a doughnut from the glass case. "What'll you have?" she asked Nick.

"The same. That'll do for a start," he told the clerk, then added milk, a couple of packaged burritos and ham sandwiches. "No mustard," he whispered as he brushed past her to heat the frozen burritos in the microwave.

The clerk added Nick's purchases to the tab, then counted the change into Dee's hand as Nick reached for his wallet. "Think you're tricky, don't you?" he said.

She shrugged. "It was my turn." Before he had a chance to say anything else, she gathered up her share of the food and headed for the truck.

By the time they reached the rodeo grounds, her stomach had reached a full, rumbling roar as it reacted to the smell of food. She almost wished she'd gotten one of the burritos, but she knew it wouldn't taste as good as it smelled. The packaged ones never did.

Dee did a double-take as she followed Nick into the tiny trailer. "It's clean!" she commented, unable to keep the surprise from her voice.

"I had to do something while I waited for you to wake up. Just don't open the closet, whatever you do," he warned.

"Fibber McGee's, right?" She teased back. "I'd forgotten about that." She smiled as she remembered the old radio show broadcast on Saturday mornings by the local radio station. Fibber McGee and Molly, W.C. Fields, George Burns, and all the others had added a little old-fashioned, corny humor to the morning chores, thanks to the radio in the barn.

"Matt and I use some of their jokes."

"I guess that shouldn't surprise me," she replied. She opened her bag and started on a plump doughnut.

They ate in silence, then tucked the leftovers into the trailer refrigerator. Nick wiped the crumbs from the table, then pulled out the case that held his clown makeup.

"Can I watch? Or will that make you nervous?" Dee asked.

He looked unperturbed as he opened the case and positioned the mirror. "No cracks about mascara and false eyelashes."

"You take all the fun out of it." She settled herself back into the chair opposite him and watched, fascinated while he smeared on white and red. His calloused fingers moved with practiced, efficient strokes, smoothing and evening the color, outlining the smile, and adding the marks around his eyes. Dee leaned back while he dusted the finished product with powder to set the makeup. The entire process took less than three minutes.

"You're pretty quiet," he said as he packed his supplies away. She couldn't read his expression behind the makeup, but his eyes didn't meet hers.

"I was afraid I'd make you mess up. One slip of the pencil and you'd have to start over. I hate to think what sort of revenge you'd take for that," she teased.

His shoulders relaxed as an easy grin blended into the painted one.

"Let's get this over with so I can take this stuff off. It itches," he commented.

While Nick went in search of his friends, Dee made her way directly across the field toward the arena. Once she reached the bleachers, she opened the camera bag and began to assemble the gear she'd need.

By the time she had loaded the camera and snapped on the zoom lens, Nick and two other cowboys were herding a half dozen steers through the gate to the arena. She recognized the grizzled older cowboy from last night. The younger one was a stranger. Tucking a couple of extra rolls of film into her pocket, she let herself into the arena and joined them at the gate.

"Well, hello again," the younger cowboy said, holding out a calloused hand.

Dee squinted against the sun in her face, trying to remember if she'd ever met him. His voice was familiar, but she couldn't quite place him. He obviously recognized her, she thought as his fingers squeezed hers lightly.

"Matt Godwin," Nick supplied when she turned questioning eyes to him. "He's the barrel man."

"The guy with the bad sense of humor," she said, softening the dig with a wink.

Quick on the uptake, Matt winked back. "See, Nick? I told you she'd be a good sport about it."

Nick shook his head. "Sure. *Now* she's a good sport. Last night I thought she was going to punch me."

"I nearly did," Dee admitted.

The old cowboy chuckled and patted her on the shoulder as he passed. "You watch out for them two," he said. "They're nothin' but trouble when you get them together."

Nick released a long-suffering sigh. "I ought to fire you, Pete."

"Yeah, yeah, yeah," Pete said, moving toward the huddle of steers in a stiff trot. "Which one of these you want first?"

"Run the bald-faced one this way when I give you the signal," Nick yelled back, then waited for Dee to adjust the settings on the camera and position herself.

She shot two rolls of film from the ground while the three men choreographed a series of turnbacks, dodges, and close passes. Then she climbed to the top of a tall, sturdy fence post. Wrapping her legs around the woven wire to balance herself, she shot another roll from that angle.

She'd just loaded more film when she glanced up to catch an unguarded look on Nick's face. Her fingers faltered on the camera back to the brief glimpse of warm possessiveness in his eyes. She blinked, and it was gone.

Dee mentally shook herself. She was letting her imagination run away with her again. Then he smiled, and her chest swelled with breath-stealing emotion.

"Ready?" he asked in a perfectly normal tone.

Calling herself ten times a fool, she pulled herself

together. At her nod, he spun and signaled the others to send yet another steer his way.

Then he glanced back over his shoulder at her. This time their eyes met and held, sending a wild heat searing through Dee's veins. It spun through her body, then settled into frantic throbbing. Then a shout broke the spell.

Nick caught sight of the steer bearing down on him and darted to the left. Then he tripped. Dee watched in panicked fear as he scooted, then rolled away from the steer's hooves in a maneuver so slick and automatic it seemed rehearsed. Except she knew it wasn't.

"Good thing that wasn't old Devil Eater. He'd have stomped you into the mud," Pete called out as Nick picked himself up.

"Naw, I planned it that way," Nick shouted back. He took a step, hesitated, then bent over and adjusted his shoelaces. He stopped tying twice to rub his ankle. Then he rose slowly, stepping carefully her way.

"You get that on film?" he asked.

"I'll send you a print," she murmured, still shaken. "Are you all right?" She didn't care about the photos anymore. All she could see was Nick's body rolling away from the pounding hooves. And this was only a young steer, less than half the size of the bulls he would face tonight.

He squinted up at her, narrowing his eyes. "I'm fine. I do this all the time, remember?"

"I thought maybe you'd hurt your leg or your ankle. You acted like it bothered you."

He winked, and her already quivering stomach felt like it had turned over. "You were watching that closely, were you?"

Dee arched her brows, matching his mischievous expression with what she hoped was a repressive one of her own. "Artists notice little details like that. So what *is* wrong with your leg?"

The laughing glints in his eyes disappeared. Even though his smile remained, she sensed his withdrawal. "Just a twinge," he said. "Ready for some more?"

"I have enough," Dee replied, dipping her head as she lifted the camera strap from around her neck.

"I'm fine," he repeated in a low voice, then aimed a shout in Pete's direction. "Run that bald-faced rascal back up here."

The older cowboy lifted his head from the pattern he was scratching in the dirt with his boot toe. "What was that again?" he shouted back.

"Never mind," she called, swinging the camera out to gently tap Nick on the shoulder until he glanced back her way. "Take this so I can get down from here. My legs are getting stiff and I think I might have a splinter in an uncomfortable place."

His fingers closed around the camera strap and his other arm came up to steady her. "Sorry," he said. "You should have said something sooner."

She pursed her lips, sending him a speaking glance before climbing carefully down and taking the camera back.

"How about some shots from the chute gates?" Nick suggested.

Dee hesitated, not wanting to push the issue. But she hadn't imagined that limping first step, or the careful way he was moving now. Pete must have seen it, too, because he strode over and clapped Nick on the shoulder. "What do you say we give those rascals a rest? If we run all the vinegar out of them now, they won't be any challenge at all for the show tonight." His words were light, but there was a stern message in his eyes when he looked at Dee.

She nodded carefully in acknowledgment and slipped

the camera strap over her shoulder. "My thoughts exactly. Anyone else here dying for a cold drink?"

"Don't drink the water here," Pete warned. "Smells like rotten eggs and tastes worse."

Dee chuckled. "I'll remember that," she replied, adding her thanks for helping with the photo shoot.

She packed her gear while the men herded the animals back through the gate and into their pen. By the time she'd finished, Nick had disappeared. She looked around for a few minutes, then decided he must have gone back to the trailer to clean up. Or maybe he considered the job finished and had gone on to other business. The thought left a familiar hollow feeling in her midsection. But she hadn't imagined that bone-melting look, had she? Shaking her head, she decided this place was a bad influence. She'd be fine once she returned to her airy house and her drawing board. It was just the rodeo atmosphere and all the memories that gave her these crazy thoughts.

She was halfway back to the trailer when Matt caught up with her.

"There you are," he called as he fell into step beside her. "I looked around and you were gone. I'm supposed to tell you to meet Nick at the truck. He'll be there as soon as he changes and cleans his face up a bit."

Dee smiled softly as a warm flood of feeling swept through her. "No problem," she replied, watching the rough ground at her feet. "I'm already headed in that direction."

"Yeah, umm . . . there's one other thing."

His hesitant tone surprised her. He'd gone from casual messenger to awkward schoolboy in a matter of seconds. "What is it?" she asked, then stopped next to a red horse trailer when he did.

"Well, two things, really," he began. "First, I want

to apologize for last night, the joke and all, and for leaving you at the trailer alone. Nick wasn't too happy with me about that, and he was right. Nobody I know would've laid a hand on you, but sometimes there's a few strangers hanging around back here, local lowlife and the like."

Dee suppressed a smile. "I live in the city, Matt. I know how to deal with lowlife."

"I'm not sayin' you don't—"

"What else?" she prompted gently.

He adjusted his hat again, then turned an intent gaze on her. "You're just here for the rodeo, just for this book, right?"

She straightened, meeting his gaze head-on. She had an idea where he was leading, but she wanted to wait and be sure. No doubt Matt had heard stories about the rotten deal Tony had gotten from Dee's mother, unfounded rumors that floated about unconfirmed, but spreading nonetheless. "That's why Craig and I came," was all she said.

"And Nick?"

"He's an old friend. It's good to see him again."

He nodded slowly. "Keep it that way. Don't go messing with his head."

"I'm not sure what you're implying."

"Don't try to kid me," he replied in a low, warning tone. "You're a smart woman. Smart and pretty. You know exactly what I'm saying. Distractions can kill a man in this line of work. Don't be one."

Dee lowered her eyes. Had she distracted Nick this afternoon? Was that why he'd nearly been stomped by the steer? She looked up at his partner and saw her doubts mirrored in his expression.

"Is that what happened?" she asked, abandoning all pretense.

He shrugged. "Who knows?" Without another word,

he left her alone. She watched him make his way to the gate and disappear in the maze of cattle pens and board fences on the other side.

Only then did she continue on toward the truck. Nick was just stepping out of the trailer when she approached.

"Matt been talking your ear off?" he asked.

Dee shook her head. "I took my time. I figured it would take you a while to remove the greasepaint."

He shook his head. "I've got it down to two minutes flat. Of course, that's a rough job."

"I can tell," she replied, reaching up to wipe a smudge of white at his hairline.

His easy grin faltered when she touched him, and she withdrew her fingers self-consciously. He captured her hand before she could draw away completely, then lifted it to his lips. She felt the barest brush of warmth on her palm. It was enough to double her heart rate.

"Soft," he said, tracing the lines of her palm with his fingertips. "Smooth and soft." A brief shadow crossed his face.

Dee realized then the meaning of bittersweet. He stirred her more powerfully than any man she'd ever met. These feelings were every bit as intense as her first adolescent crush on him, only now the emotions had matured. Only she was no longer an innocent child. She was a mature woman with mature needs, and she knew very well what her body's response meant. Yet they'd done no more than touch, except for that one brief kiss. Anything more was unwise. She couldn't forget what had happened to Tony and Pam. And she couldn't forget what Matt had said.

SEVEN

Dee forced herself to laugh, then winced at the sound. She'd meant it to be light and uncaring, and instead it came out harsh and uneasy. "Paintbrushes don't build that many calluses," she commented.

"I guess not." Nick dropped her hands and turned away, pulling the truck keys out of his pocket. "Come on. I'll give you a ride back."

She nodded slowly and followed him to the truck. A chill replaced the warm fuzzy feeling. She felt shut out, and it was awful. It shouldn't matter, but it did.

Nick remained silent for the brief drive back to the motel, and she didn't dare ask him what had caused his sudden mood change. She knew. In that bare moment, before she'd thought to shield her expression, he'd glimpsed her desire. In her eyes, on her face, in the shallowness of her breath—what did it matter. He'd pulled away because he didn't feel the same. She closed her eyes in silent embarrassment, wishing she could just disappear. Then the truck bounced through the rough entrance to the motel parking lot.

She was already opening her door when the truck rolled to a stop near her motel room. "Thanks for the ride and the photos. I'll send you some copies when I get them developed. You are still at the same address, aren't you? Or do you have a card or something with the right address?'' Grabbing her bag, she slid off the seat to the ground.

Nick cleared his throat. ''Dee? I—never mind.''

His puzzled tone halted her. A tiny hope flared in her and she peered into the truck.

''What?''

''It's nothing.'' He wouldn't look at her. His fingers drummed nervously on the dashboard.

Nervous? Nick? ''What were you going to say?'' she insisted.

He hesitated a moment longer, then turned a tentative smile on her. ''What did you have planned for this afternoon?'' he asked.

''Nothing much. I thought I might wander around, maybe make a few sketches, take a few pictures. Why?'' She tilted her head to one side, wondering what he was thinking.

''I need to drive out and look over a colt that's for sale near here. I could use a second opinion.''

She didn't bother to hide her surprise. ''You're kidding? Why not take Matt or Pete?''

''They've already seen him.''

''And what did they say?''

''Matt recommends I buy him. Pete wasn't sure.''

''And you want my opinion? That's a first,'' she answered in a mildly sarcastic tone.

''Is that a no?''

''Not necessarily.''

The corner of Nick's smile twitched as the warmth seeped back into his eyes. ''Would you like to come?'' he repeated.

She considered for a moment. She'd love to, both to see the horse and to spend a little more time with this man she was beginning to know again. Matt's warning jangled in her brain, but she brushed it away. It was ridiculous, the idea that Nick thought about her enough to become distracted from his work. He wasn't that interested or that stupid. The near miss this afternoon had been a fluke, a weird coincidence. And her reaction to him? Well, she'd figure that one out later.

"What time?" she asked.

"How about now?"

Dee shrugged, trying to control her excitement and barely succeeding. "Sounds fine to me. What about the camera?"

"Bring it along. If this one is as good as they say, I might ask you to take a few photos for me. I'd pay for them, of course."

She grinned and shoved the camera bag across the seat to him. "Carry this and the pictures are on the house."

It took nearly half an hour to reach the farm, but she was no closer to knowing what was happening between them. They'd talked, but about impersonal things such as the weather and the price of pickup trucks.

The farm itself was nothing special, a small white house and a bigger white barn. But the colt skittering about behind that barn was something else entirely. All fire and lightning-fast movement, it agilely avoided them until Nick took a bucket of sweet feed mix to the pasture and shook it. The little devil flicked its tail, stretched out its neck, and sniffed. Nick shook the bucket again until the colt crowded up next to its mother and nibbled on the grain mix.

Speaking softly and moving with deceptive nonchalance, Nick slipped a rope around the colt's neck and coaxed it up to the fence. Surprisingly enough, it followed easily, finished with its game of tag.

Dee stayed back while Nick looked over the colt

from nose to tail, then checked its legs and hooves. She caught his signal and climbed the fence, camera in hand. The first click of the shutter startled the colt, but he settled down quickly under Nick's stroking hand.

She wasn't sure what kind of pictures Nick wanted, so she shot from several different angles. Then he and the farmer began to talk business.

"Come on into the house and have a cold drink while we sort this out," the man suggested.

"Sounds good," Nick agreed as he unsnapped the lead and set the colt free. It strolled nonchalantly around the corner of the barn and back, then whickered impatiently. An answering neigh from the mare grazing farther up the hill put speed in his hooves as he thundered across the field.

"I think I'll stay out here and watch the horses, if you don't mind," Dee said.

"If you want," the man said. "Sure you wouldn't like something cold to drink, a sandwich or something?"

"Thanks, but I'm fine," she said. She watched the men make their way to the house, her eyes lingering on Nick's strong back, then lower at his legs as she searched for a sign of his earlier limp. His gait appeared sound and sure.

"Sound and sure," she muttered with a grimacing shake of her head. You'd think she was talking about a horse. She was falling back under the Ramsey influence in more ways than one. Already, she'd slipped into old patterns of thought and speech.

A movement on the hillside caught her attention, and she turned back to watch the colt scamper about and beleaguer its mother. Then she noticed a fluffy kitten chasing a butterfly through a nearby bed of tall black-eyed Susans. It followed the insect through the fence and into the pasture. Then the colt charged down hill with the mare on his heels, nipping lightly at his hindquarters, no doubt in retaliation for some infraction.

The kitten halted, the butterfly forgotten. Dee held her breath, expecting the kitten to be crushed beneath the hard, battering hooves. The tiny fluff of fur charged fearlessly and leaped. Somehow the kitten clung to the mare's tail, catching her claws in the coarse, tangled hair. The kitten fell free after a moment, then positioned itself for another charge. Laughing to herself, Dee pulled out the camera and finished the roll of film while the kitten took two more rides. She'd just changed the film and stored the camera back in the bag when the men returned.

"Ready?" Nick asked, coming up beside her.

"Whenever you are. Did you see that yellow kitten?" she asked, turning to the farmer. "I've never seen a cat catch a ride in a horse's tail before."

He shook his head. "Crazy cat's going to get killed. It was born a bit stupid, wouldn't you say?"

Dee shrugged. "Maybe it just has a bigger sense of adventure than other cats. Like skydivers and mountain climbers," she said.

The farmer fixed her with a skeptical grin. "Like I said, born a bit stupid. If it weren't for my wife, I'd—"

A loud clatter from a bell mounted near the back door halted his words. "And I'll bet that's her now. she knows I'm talking about her. I'd better get that," he said, backing away. "Nice meetin' you, ma'am, and I'll see you before the end of the summer, if not sooner, Nick."

A few seconds later, the man disappeared into the house, and the two of them turned back toward the truck. "Well?" she prompted. "Did you buy the colt?"

Nick grinned. "Do you think I should have?"

"How should I know? I think he's adorable. I don't suppose that counts for much."

Nick snorted. "Come on. I taught you better than that. Don't tell me you've forgotten." His voice held a challenge she couldn't resist.

"O-kay," she began, drawing out the word while she marshaled her thoughts. "He had good legs and a real tight turn. His neck's too short. He might make a good stock horse, but I don't know how he'd be for breeding. Depends on what you wanted to get out of him. How's that?"

He stopped, hands on hips, and graced her with a wide, pleased smile. "Not bad. You forgot his fetlocks and hooves."

She sauntered on up to the truck. "I wasn't close enough to see," she flung over her shoulder as nonchalantly as she could manage around her pleasure with his mild praise.

"Guess!" His boots crunched in the gravel behind her as she opened the door and climbed inside. His hand on the door prevented her from closing it. "Go on, take a shot," he prompted.

"Good. You were smiling."

His brows rose skeptically. "No, I wasn't. If I'd been smiling, the old man would've asked three hundred more."

"You were, too. Those little lines around your eyes crinkle, even if you won't let your lips smile. Like now," she retorted. "I saw it. You like that colt. I'm right, aren't I?"

"You're right," he admitted. "I bought him. I'll pick him up next month on the way back through from Oklahoma City to Des Moines." His warm, longing expression warned her that his thoughts had already left the colt. The glance lasted no more than a second.

but it was enough to stir the banked fires into glowing embers.

"You'll be back that soon?" Dee's voice was husky, even to her own ears. The tension in hazy heat of the truck cab simmered around her until she felt a tremble that would have toppled her if she'd been standing. The idea of being more than passing ships took root and refused to be dismissed.

Nick saw the roiling confusion, the bared emotions that darkened her eyes. "Don't look at me that way," he said. "Not when I don't dare touch you."

Her sharp intake of breath sliced through his gut like a knife. "Damn!" he muttered through clenched teeth when she turned away from him, holding herself stiff and erect as she stared straight ahead. He pushed the door closed with gentle regret, wishing it wasn't already too late for them. Wishing he didn't still want her so badly he ached, so badly he'd ignored his better judgment and grasped at the chance to keep her by his side for a few hours more. Slowly, he made his way to the driver's seat and turned the key. The engine responded with a low, well-tuned hum, but he barely noticed.

Dee didn't look at him, didn't speak for a long moment. "I don't understand," she finally said in a low, controlled voice. Her face was a cool mask, but her fingers fidgeted with the strap of the camera bag, betraying her agitation.

"I'd want more," he said baldly. "It's always been that way. And after all these years, the wanting is still there. Only there's no good end to it, is there?"

Dee paled, but her expression never faltered. Only a faint flicker in her eyes gave a clue that she'd heard him. "You never said anything."

"You were fifteen."

"I grew up."

He nodded slowly. "I noticed." Her pallor changed

to a flush as his eyes took in the changes ten years had wrought. He had no doubt that he liked what he saw. She stirred him more deeply than any woman he'd ever known. But they'd become so different. His father and Pam had shown them by example what happens when two vastly different people try to make a life together.

He groaned when her hand brushed his cheek in a light caress. He captured the fingers and kissed them lightly, one by one, unable to help himself. Then his lips touched hers and he breathed in her soft sigh. She tasted sweet and warm and so full of promise that he ached for what he didn't dare take. Then her tongue touched his. He tasted fire. Hot, melting desire hardened his body and made him wish it was dark, that they were someplace besides the cramped bench seat of a pickup truck.

When he drew her closer still, his knee banged against the stick shift, and the pain brought him back to his senses. Drawing a deep, shuddering breath, he eased back and released her as she pulled away and reached silently for the seat belt. She looked as stunned as he felt.

"I won't apologize," he told her.

"Don't you dare, Nick Ramsey," she retorted, staring straight ahead. "Now tell me about this new colt of yours. What are you going to do with him?"

It was late afternoon by the time they got back to the rodeo grounds. Already, a few scattered cars and pickup trucks dotted the field set aside for general parking.

"Are you going back tonight or tomorrow?" Nick asked as they drove through the opened gate.

"Tomorrow. Craig doesn't like to drive after dark if he can help it. Night blindness. And he can't stand for anyone else to drive, either."

"Can't say I blame him, although I'd guess your driving skills have improved somewhat since the barn incident."

"That wasn't my fault," Dee pointed out, barely able to suppress a laugh. The steering pin on the tractor she'd been driving had snapped. The tractor crashed hard into the side of the barn, demolishing a four-foot section of wall and the feedbox on the other side.

His hand closed over hers where it lay on the vinyl seat, then he winked conspiratorially. "Did anyone ever tell you about my first tractor ride?"

Dee laughed. "You're a little late with your moral support. After you finished yelling at me and stalked off, Tony told me about the time you drove into the pond."

"He did?" He seemed surprised. "He never mentioned it."

"I guess he figured knowing it would make me feel better. And it did."

"Well, I guess I shouldn't have yelled at you that way. It seems like I was always yelling at you when I guess I was really scared you'd hurt yourself."

She laced her fingers through his and squeezed. "Or I did something dumb or kept bugging you. I guess it must have been a real pain having an instant little sister who knew nothing about horses, or cattle, or the weird noises animals make at night."

"I never thought of you as my sister," he pointed out, pulling his hand to his lips and planting a kiss in her palm. The simple action sent tingles up her arm, tightening her breasts in response and igniting tiny fires along the path and beyond. The affectionate gesture gave new meaning to his words. For the first time, they carried no sting. Instead, they warmed her, even while they confused her.

"How did you think of me?" she asked, searching

his expression for the truth. He stared straight ahead, watching the bumpy road and slowing as a pair of riders slipped in front of them, then crossed to the other side and into the grassy space behind the bleachers.

Finally, he spoke. "Dance with me again tonight, and I'll tell you."

"Chicken," she accused.

He shook his head. "Now isn't the time."

"When is a good time? I'm leaving tomorrow, and for all I know you could be leaving as soon as the rodeo is over."

"Nope. First thing tomorrow morning. I have to be in Denver by Wednesday, and there's a couple of stops I need to make along the way."

"Horses?"

"What else?"

What indeed? It could be a thousand things, she knew so little about his life now. The thought gave her pause. She really didn't know him, not anymore. And she tried to tell herself it didn't matter. She was here to do a job. Meeting Nick again was just an interesting coincidence. But a vague sense of loss pervaded her as she stared out the window.

Dee scanned the grounds for Craig as they drove past the arena and through the next set of gates. She spotted him close by, swinging a lariat awkwardly above his head. A group of children milled around him, some practicing with their own ropes, some watching, and a couple wrestling on the ground. The others, spotting Nick's truck, hurried over, clamoring for his attention.

Casting her an apologetic look, he turned off the key. "Sorry, I promised them a lesson today. Looks like they caught me."

She shook her head. "No, I should be the one who's sorry. I've taken up too much of your time already today. Go on with the kids and I'll go rescue Craig."

Nick cast her a skeptical look before glancing back over his shoulder and chuckled. "That crew would wear out anybody." He shook his head in resignation when the youngsters reached the truck and started speaking in a jumble. "Catching anything?" Nick called out the window as Craig drew closer, trailing tiredly behind the children. The clamor quieted to a mild roar as Nick opened the truck door and climbed out.

"A few laughs," Craig replied. "Roping's harder than it looks, but I guess you know that. That little tyke in the big hat does better than me."

Dee followed Craig's pointing finger to the redheaded boy and watched him swing the rope deftly above his head. Then he let the rope zing toward the bale, snagging one end.

"Nice," she muttered to herself, remembering her own attempts at roping practice. Either she'd been a poor learner or the bale had moved around quite a bit. In any case, Nick had soon given up and had put her in the saddle instead. Then he'd taught her how to separate a calf from its mother and how to move an uncooperative cow out of the underbrush and through a gate. And she hadn't been half bad at that, either, although she had to admit that the horse did most of the work. All she'd really had to do was stay in the saddle.

When Nick and the children headed for the practice bales, Dee joined Craig at the tailgate. "You look tired, old man. What do you say we go find some food? I can eat and you can prop your feet up and rest."

Craig tugged her ponytail and smirked as he took her arm. "I want to watch Nick for a minute. From what I heard today, he doesn't miss his calf very often."

Dee let Craig pull her over to where Nick was working with the kids. "I spent a lot of time sitting on a board fence and watching him and his friends practice.

He used to be pretty good. How he got into bull riding instead is beyond me," she commented as they walked.

"He still is good," Craig whispered. "I heard that last night is the first time he's missed in three months. And that black gelding of his is a top-notch stock horse."

"Last night?" She halted in her tracks. "At the rodeo? He still competes? And what's this about a horse? He has a horse with him? Where does he put it? On the couch?"

Craig turned, a startled expression on his face. "How should I know? Somebody hauls it for him, I guess."

"And what else did you find out?" she demanded.

Craig stared down at her. "You didn't know? What did the two of you talk about all afternoon?"

Dee started to speak, then her jaw slackened as a slow flush crept up her neck. She'd spent the better part of the day with the man, and she still hadn't learned as much as Craig had picked up in hearsay. She knew about the ranch, about his horse-breeding operation and the stock horses.

But she hadn't known he was still competing or that he brought his horse with him. It made sense, though. It explained where he'd been while she waited in his trailer last night for the smiling clown to appear. It explained the hastily removed makeup on the towel and the traces still along his hairline when he'd finally appeared. But Craig's information painted a different picture of Nick than she'd imagined. It added a depth that was as puzzling as it was enlightening.

Her gaze strayed to Nick, where he crouched next to a small pig-tailed girl and adjusted her grip on the rope. He glanced up at that instant and smiled warmly. Dee's lips curved automatically in answer. Then he winked and turned his attention back to the child, guiding her gently through the motion of the swing, talking low and steady all the while. When the rope landed on the end of the bale, the girl squealed and leaped into his arms for a big hug.

"Dee? What's going on with the two of you?" Craig's gaze narrowed suspiciously.

Dee turned away. "Nothing. We went to see a colt. I took pictures of it. He bought it. We came back. End of story."

"Right. Well, you can tell me about it or not. It's your business."

She glanced back at him and sighed. "It's no big deal. I was just surprised, that's all."

"I was surprised, too. But evidently it's not that unusual for the clowns to compete in other events, the calf roping or team roping usually. Matt says Nick loans out his horse, too, for a share of the prize money. He must be doing pretty well, better than most of these guys is the impression I got."

Dee nodded absently. "Probably. Craig, give me a minute, will you?" Not waiting for an answer, she joined Nick and tapped him lightly on the arm.

"Do you mind if I leave the camera bag in your truck? I'll pick it up before the rodeo tonight."

"No problem. Or better yet," he added, digging into his pocket and pulling out his keys. "Why don't you just take the truck? I won't need it this evening."

When she hesitated, he pressed the keys into her hand. "You only have a couple of hours. Why waste half of it walking between here and the motel?" he reasoned. His warm, calloused fingers clung to her soft, small hand for an instant, then he pushed her gently toward the truck.

"The rodeo starts at seven," he reminded her.

"Where will you be?"

He shrugged. "Around. Just leave the truck by the trailer if you can't find me."

"Before I forget, what about the photos of the colt? Where should I send the prints?" she called over her shoulder.

He shrugged. "We'll talk about it later. Why don't you meet me at the trailer after the rodeo?"

Dee nodded her assent. There were questions she wanted answered, for her own peace of mind, if nothing else. So why did the idea of meeting him alone at his trailer stir up a nest of butterflies in her stomach? And why did she even think they would be alone, she added as she and Craig left Nick and the children behind. In her experience, nobody was alone after the rodeo's end. Everyone was somewhere, celebrating or commiserating, unless they were already on the road to the next rodeo.

Two hours later, after a refreshing shower and a mouth-watering steak, they returned to the rodeo grounds just as the rodeo was about to begin.

For most of the rodeo, they sat among a group of rodeo wives who had taken over a section of the bleachers near the chutes. The red-haired imp from that afternoon recognized Craig immediately and climbed into his lap. Looking slightly uncomfortable, Craig bounced the child awkwardly, then coaxed him onto the bench beside him.

"Tyler, you get back down here," a harried young woman called from the front row. "I'm sure the poor man has seen enough of you already today."

"It's okay," Craig called. "He's welcome to sit here, if you don't mind."

The woman frowned, then shot out an arm to corral a boisterous toddler who was venturing too close to the arena fence. "You're sure?"

Craig nodded. "Tye's teaching me how to rope," he added. The woman smiled gratefully as she pulled the toddler onto her lap, then turned to chastise twin girls only slightly older than Tye.

"Well, send him down if he gets to be a nuisance," the woman said.

Soon afterward, Dee moved farther down the arena to better position herself for the roping events. Crouching low so she wouldn't block anyone's view, she shot most of a roll on the calf ropers before she heard Nick's name over the loudspeaker. This time, he didn't miss, and his team's time was good enough to place them second in the money.

Then it was time for the final event of the night, the second heat of the bull riding. Dee's knees suddenly began to quiver. Knowing she wouldn't be in any condition to take a decent photo, she made her way back to Craig while Nick and Matt filled the time between the events with corny jokes.

Once she caught Matt watching her, and when he started her way, she held up a threatening fist. Seeing it, the clown grinned wider and turned in search of some other victim for his pranks.

Dee slid on to the seat next to Craig, noting that Pete now sat on the other side.

"Where's your buddy?" she asked once she was settled. She shoved the camera bag onto the bench beside her and tried to quell her nervousness.

Pete snickered. "The cotton-candy man came by."

"I wasn't very interesting anymore," Craig replied in a dry tone. "You see I—"

She lost the rest of what he said. The chute gate opened and Nick sprang into action, turning the bull and sending it into a spin. She barely noticed the rider. When it was over, she sagged back with relief and exchanged a quivering smile with Pete.

Before she could recover completely, it began all over again. And it was ten times worse than last night.

Now she feared for Nick. Every time the chute gate opened she saw only him, taunting, slapping, and spinning away from the massive head, the battering hooves.

That last ride was a short one, with the rider slipping off to the side and down almost immediately.

"Down in the well," Pete muttered.

Fear stabbed at her midsection. Instead of falling away from the bull, the cowboy had slipped to the inside of the tight spin the bull had swung into when it left the chute. Before Dee could see whether the rider was still underfoot, Nick burst forward and popped the bull hard between the eyes, stalling the spin. The bull halted, snorted, then charged at Nick in short bursts. He sidestepped, then darted to the side and passed Matt and his barrel. She gasped when Matt ducked into his barrel and the bull butted it over. But she stopped breathing when Nick circled around and slapped the pale-gray bull's hindquarters to distract him from the barrel.

And then it was over. The bull spied the open gate that led from the arena to the pens around back, and he made his escape.

Dee sat still, drained, while the crowd around her stood and applauded, shouting their praise. The scores and standings were announced, and everyone packed up their cans, jackets, and children and started for the exits.

"Where will Nick be?" she asked Pete, catching him by the arm as he edged his way through the crowd.

"Hard to say just now. Maybe with the horses, maybe off someplace else. Why don't you wait for him back at the trailer?" he suggested. "He'll be back there to change in a bit."

She nodded, then fell back into step beside Craig as they made their way down the bleacher steps to the grassy aisle. In front of them, the red-haired boy stepped on one of the twin's heels, starting a scuffle. His mother swatted both, then hauled the toddler up into her arms and ordered the rest to stay close. A moment later, the five of them disappeared into the crowd.

Craig stopped twice to talk before they reached the back gate to the field where Nick's trailer was parked. Already restless, Dee tapped her foot impatiently then decided to go on without him.

She slipped through the gate to the back field only a few seconds after the harried mother and her four youngsters. Half amused with their sleepy stumblings, Dee trailed along behind them, walking alternately in the road, and in the grass while loaded campers and pickup trucks lumbered past them.

At first, she didn't pay any attention to the shouts from the arena. Then the crashing sound of splintering wood filled the air. She spun around to see a ghostly gray, snorting beast charging for the relatively open space of the field.

"Bull on the loose," someone shouted, and everyone scattered.

Dee started for the protection of a nearby horse trailer, then spotted the red-haired imp who had pestered Craig for the better part of the evening. Standing in the middle of the road, he stared openmouthed at the bull coming his way. Without thinking, Dee whirled back in that direction, stumbled over a rough clump of grass, then righted herself.

Behind her, she could hear more shouts and the clatter of hooves against the hard-packed dirt. She thought she heard her name, but when she turned to look, the bull was bearing down on her. Then she caught the child in her arms and leaped for the trees. As she ducked behind a rough-barked tree trunk, she thought she felt the hot breath of the bull on her neck.

For a moment there was nothing but noise—clattering, snorting, and screaming, with distinctive snap of a leather whip mingled in. Then the hoofbeats faded off into the distance. An engine that had seen better days rumbled by. Urgent voices rang out, and she recognized the frantic call of Tye's mother.

"Over here," she called, taking a tentative step out into the open.

"You okay, lady?" someone asked. Dee nodded and set the boy down. He darted out, running full force into his mother's arms, frightened tears streaming down his face.

"The bull . . ." Dee began, glancing around uneasily. She spotted Nick as he darted between the vehicles, running her way.

"Dee? You're hurt!" he exclaimed, wild-eyed in the faint light cast by a truck left idling nearby. His face was devoid of the clown smile, but deathly pale, as if he hadn't had time to wipe all the white greasepaint away. As he drew closer, Dee saw that it wasn't paint, but fear that made his freckles stand out in relief against the pallor of his skin.

"I'm okay. Where's the bull?"

"Penned up now," Nick said. He dropped an arm casually over her shoulder and touched her face. "You're bleeding." Although his touch was light, she could feel the tautness of his muscles, the tension in his voice.

"No, I'm fine," she replied, pulling away. Her limbs were shaky with reaction, but she felt a great need to stand on her own or she'd never quell the trembling. "You're sure he can't get loose again? I don't think I could do that twice," she added shakily.

She sagged back onto the ground, sitting on a low croft of grass. Craig appeared out of the darkness and dropped down beside her. "Where's the camera?" he asked.

"The camera? Who cares about the damned camera?" Nick retorted in a strangled voice, pulling Dee up against him. For an instant, she savored the closeness, then she felt the trembling start again in her limbs.

"Craig's right," she said, easing back. "I dropped it somewhere when I started running."

"It's not important," Nick insisted.

"It is. There's a whole weekend of work in that camera bag. Help me find it before someone runs over it, if they haven't already."

Searching would give her something to do, something to distract her until she overcame the shakiness. She stood before Nick could offer further protest and tried to retrace her steps. It took only a moment to locate the bag. And other than a dirty smudge on the side, it and the equipment inside seemed undamaged. Then she noticed the smear of blood on her hand.

"Where did that come from?" she muttered, staring down. Then she gingerly touched her forehead. "You're right. I am bleeding."

Craig pushed her hair back from her forehead and squinted. "Doesn't look too bad," he said. "Just a scrape. How's the kid?"

Dee grimaced and looked past him to the group huddled around Tye. "Okay, I guess. I think he's starting to enjoy this." The little boy's tear-streaked face was split by an ear-to-ear grin as he recounted his escape. Then a tall, lean man in a gray felt hat grabbed him up and clutched him close.

"Daddy," Tye shouted. "I almost caught the bull."

Dee gaped, then burst into laughter while Tye's mother sputtered, then spewed forth into a lecture that subdued the child in no uncertain terms. Then she clasped Dee's hand and thanked her profusely.

"Ungrateful brat," the woman muttered with exasperation, although a smile teased at the corner of her lips even as she spoke. "If you hadn't been there—I hate to think what would have happened."

"The little devil probably would have punched the beast between the eyes," Craig interjected, running his fingers though his silver hair. "Ma'am, I don't see how you manage it. One of those kids would do me in."

She cast a pointed look toward the man who held Tye. "This is it. This is the last time we go on the road with him," she said. "Thanks again," she added with a last squeeze to Dee's hand. "Let me know when the book comes out. I'll buy a dozen copies."

Dee stared after the family as the woman rejoined them and reached for her son. She felt a prick of envy, then pushed it away. It wasn't envy, she told herself. She was just suffering from emotional reaction. That's why her knees were starting to shake again and her teeth were chattering.

"Come on, let's see about those scratches," Craig said. When she didn't respond, he stared down. "Dee?"

"G-give m-me a ss-ec-cond," she managed to say before her knees buckled completely.

Nick caught her before she hit the ground and scooped her up. "It's all right," he whispered, clutching her close. "It's fine. It's over."

She tucked her head against his neck and shivered.

EIGHT

"Good heavens, she looks like she's going into shock," Craig exclaimed. "That head wound must be worse than it looks." He gingerly touched Dee's forehead, and she brushed his hand away with an irritated growl.

"She'll be fine," Nick said in a low, calm tone. "Dee's great in a crisis. She just falls apart afterward. Some women are like that," he added, eliciting a murmur of relieved laughter from several bystanders.

"Not Dee. Do you think the paramedics are still here?" Craig asked, looking worried.

Dee shifted in Nick's arms, nearly unbalancing them both. "I'm fine, d-damn it," she said before another shudder shook her.

"We don't need the paramedics," Nick agreed. Dee didn't, at least. He might before the night was over if things continued as they had. Either his leg would give out or his heart would stop beating from fear, permanently this time. A picture of the bull bearing down on Dee and the boy flashed through his mind. He recalled the impotent moment of knowing he couldn't reach her in time.

He tightened his arms around her as he tried to ease the two of them down to the ground without damaging his bad ankle. It ached already from holding their combined weight. He would just bend his knees and sit on the grass.

It seemed simple enough until he tried it. Halfway down, his ankle protested, the dull ache replaced by a sharp, shooting pain that brought a gasp to his lips. Then the leg folded beneath him, sending them both to the ground with a thump.

"Sorry," he muttered into her hair, then brushed his lips against the silky smoothness at the braided crown. He shifted, pulling her closer still and stroking her back until the worst of the shivering stopped.

"I've never known her to act like this, not even when that Peter Pan husband of hers—"

"Shut up," Dee said, managing to get that out quite clearly before another jag of teeth chattering began. "Both of you just sh-shut up."

"You're sure this is nerves?" Craig didn't look convinced, but at least he'd stopped pacing. She nodded, then tried to pull away. Nick pressed her head to his chest, murmuring low, soothing sounds as he touched her. He couldn't stop touching her.

Then a high-pitched squeak escaped from the woman in his arms. Startled, he loosened his grip enough to let her slip from the circle of his arms. She didn't move far away, just onto the ground next to him. But even that was too far. He hauled her up against him, and this time she didn't protest.

He realized she wasn't shaking from fear anymore, but from suppressed laughter. "This is funny?" he asked softly. He'd expected anger, even blind fury like when she'd recovered from her lapse of nerves after the calf incident. Or maybe even embarrassment. But laughter? That worried him.

"No. Yes. We look ridiculous. No wonder people are staring," she replied. She tucked her feet under her and started to rise.

With one quick movement, Nick pulled her back into his lap. "Not yet," he whispered. "No one's staring. Nobody's even paying any attention to us."

"Craig's watching."

Nick never took his eyes from the vulnerability revealed in her face. "He doesn't count."

"Don't tell him that," she replied after another giggle. "I'm sorry. Ignore me. I'll be back to normal in another minute or two." She tucked her head next to his neck and gave a small shiver as she relaxed against him. The small, trusting movement brought a lump to his throat. He pressed a light kiss to her hair.

When he glanced up, he met Craig's knowing eyes. But he didn't care what the man thought, only that she was all right. In less than twenty-four hours, she'd walked back into his life and turned it upside down. She'd turned him inside out.

He breathed deeply, savoring the sweet scent of her shampoo mixed with the odor of crushed grass. She stirred in his arms, then murmured a protest, pushing against him.

"Better now?" he asked softly.

"I will be if you'll let me breathe," she said.

"Sorry," Nick replied, loosening his hold guiltily. He'd practically squeezed the breath from her. "Are you ready to go?"

"I think so," she murmured. "My legs are still a little shaky."

"So are mine," he said, resisting the impulse to hug her tightly against him again.

"If that's a rude remark about my weight, you're going to pay for it," she retorted.

Craig snorted, and Nick looked up in surprise. He'd forgotten for a moment that the older man was there.

"Now I know she's all right," Craig said.

"Put a sock in it," Dee said, pulling away and easing to her feet. She still looked a little pale. The hand she held out to him trembled until he grasped it and levered himself upright. The paleness he could blame on the distortions of moonlight and halogen headlights, but not the trembling or the uncomfortable way she avoided his eyes. Her fear had given way to embarrassment in a big way.

Otherwise she appeared sound, aside from the scrape on her face and her rumpled, dirty clothes. Still, he wanted to pick her up and carry her to the trailer, to shut everyone else out until he'd assured himself that she really was all right.

But he knew that wasn't going to happen, not with Craig hovering protectively over her. Not that Dee herself would have permitted such a thing to happen, even if he were capable of it just now. She held herself stiffly, darting embarrassed eyes from one man to the other.

"I can't believe I did that," Dee said. "I'm sorry I just fell apart on you."

"Sorry? What for? I didn't know you had it in you. You were magnificent," Craig said.

"Then why do my knees feel like cooked noodles?" she commented, raising one finely lined brow.

"Now isn't important. You were great when it mattered," Craig said, obviously trying to comfort her. When he laid an arm across her shoulder, Nick felt a stab of jealousy that had nothing to do with reason. He knew that he had nothing to be jealous of as far as Craig was concerned. He also knew that he had no right to be jealous. But it didn't stop him from wanting her to himself in some private place where he could hold her close until his own fears faded.

"You okay now, kid?" he heard Craig ask for what seemed the hundredth time.

"Yes," Dee repeated, in a tone that bordered on exasperation. "You don't need to wait for me."

"Well, I'd arranged to meet somebody over at Frank's, but that can wait until we get that cut looked at."

She touched her hand to her forehead and winced. "I think I'll just borrow a mirror and Nick's first-aid kit and see to it myself. You go on. Maybe I'll see you over there later. Although after all of this excitement, I think maybe I'd better make an early night of it."

"Not a bad idea," Nick agreed. "You go on ahead. I'll look after her."

Craig only hesitated a moment before he agreed, although she figured that her threatening look probably hastened his retreat. Hitching a ride in a passing pickup truck, he was on his way with no more than a quick look over his shoulder. Then he was lost in the darkness and probably already asking questions, she decided.

A few minutes later, she stared at her reflection in Nick's makeup mirror. Now, with the evidence reflected back at her, she understood why both men had been so concerned. She looked like something out of a horror film. The blood smears alone were something from a Norman Bates nightmare. Aside from that, she was dirty from head to toe, muddy in some parts, she noticed. Funny, she didn't remember falling, or even scraping her forehead. But everything had happened so quickly.

She was alone in the trailer for the moment, waiting for Nick to return from the truck with the first-aid kit. She started toward the bathroom to clean up, but before she'd gone two steps she heard someone just outside the door. Nick's expression twisted with worry as he came back inside.

"Got everything we need, right here," he said, plunking a large, battered case down on the table and opening it up. Dee felt her eyes widen at the well-stocked first-aid kit, which appeared to include everything from surgical thread to horse-size hypodermic needles.

"I see you carry an ample supply," she commented. "But don't think you're going to use any of that stuff on me. Just give me a little soap and water and a tube of antibiotic ointment."

"It's me or the emergency room, although personally I think that scrape is mostly show," he pointed out. Then his smile curved wider and a mischievous twinkle entered his eyes. "Come on over here. I'll show you something really scary." Taking her hand, he tugged her back to the table and reached for the mirror.

"You're obnoxious, you know that? There's nothing wrong with me that soap won't cure," she retorted with a light chuckle that died when he began rummaging through the medical supplies.

"Not a chance," she added when his fingers paused on a package of surgical needles. Even the twinkle in his eye didn't warm the sudden chill she felt. Why did he feel the need to carry such an extensive supply? Obviously, he didn't intend to depend on the paramedics for on-the-spot doctoring. How often did he need to dip into that bag to patch himself up?

"This looks like an emergency room in a box," she commented, forcing an offhand tone.

He glanced up and grinned. "Not really. Just the standard first-aid stuff for us and the horses. Don't worry, I save the needles for the horses."

He tossed a bag of cotton balls on the table, then

pushed her gently into her seat. "Just sit there. I'll take care of it."

"I'd rather not," she replied, reaching for the bottle of peroxide.

"I insist." He pulled it out of her reach, then tossed her a towel. "For drips," he explained as he began sponging her forehead with a cool, wet cloth.

"You do this often?" she commented.

"Often enough," he replied noncommittally. "Sit still."

She tried, but his nearness made her jittery. His tautly muscled leg pressed against her thigh, heating her flesh through the cloth of her jeans. She could feel the warmth of him as he leaned closer. He shifted, his knee nudging higher, teasing her suddenly skittish nerves until she jerked.

"Am I hurting you?"

Dee drew a deep, shaky breath. "Not really. Just a twinge now and then." A stream of peroxide escaped the cotton ball in Nick's hand and oozed down the side of her face.

"Sorry," he offered. "Keep your eyes closed. I'll let you know when it's over."

"No nasty surprises?"

"None. I promise. Trust me."

She hesitated, then eased her lids closed again. *Trust me.* She did, with the peroxide at least. Her heart was another matter. She tried to relax, but the tantalizing brushes of denim against denim stirred thoughts that had nothing to do with first aid. It was insane, this tensing desire that was wiping out all sense of reality.

Then his fingers combed through her hair, probing for further injuries. She could have told him there weren't any, but his touch felt so good. He massaged her scalp until her head was too heavy to hold upright. The sting of the cut faded into the background as other, stronger feelings took over. Still she forced herself to keep her eyes closed, even when she heard him rattling around in the case.

"I guess it's just the one spot." His voice was faintly husky, and she couldn't resist the smile that stole on to her lips. He wasn't as unaffected as he pretended.

The faint icy sting of the antiseptic forced her eyes open again as she gritted her teeth to keep from squealing.

"Almost done," he said when she flinched. With careful hands, he taped on a gauze bandage, then held up a mirror.

The last streaks of dried blood were gone. Other than the stark white patch on her forehead, the only remaining clue to her adventure was a broken blade of grass in her hair. She plucked that away, then glanced up to find him watching her with a shuttered expression.

"Here," he said, thrusting a styrofoam cup into her hand.

Dee stared down at the amber liquid, giving a tentative sniff. "Whew! What's this? Liquid lightning?"

"False courage," he replied, then tipped up a cup of his own. "You scared the breath out of me back there," he added when he'd emptied it.

"I wasn't feeling so good myself," she said. She frowned at her reflection, then took a tentative sip of the liquor and gasped.

"Jack Daniels. Good for what ails you, Tony always said," Nick reminded her.

"Medicinally, of course," she added hoarsely. "How could I have forgotten?" She hadn't actually. A shot of whiskey had been Tony's cure for anything from a strong cough to the bouts of after-the-event panic like she'd experienced a little while ago. In between times, the bottle had sat high in the kitchen cabinet, untouched except for an occasional shot for friends during a serious game of cards. Despite his faults, alcohol was a vice Tony had generally avoided. She had to give him credit for that.

"You're a lot like him, you know," she commented.

"Tony? I guess so." A shadow crossed his expression, and Dee glanced away, suddenly uncomfortable with the subject. Why had she said that? Why remind him of reasons why they shouldn't get along when they were doing just fine?

"I meant that he used to make me feel better when I'd done something dumb. I guess you picked up the technique," she explained, then wondered whether she should have kept her mouth shut.

"What you did *was* dumb. You could have been trampled to death," He set his styrofoam cup on the counter and reached for the bottle again, then set it aside.

"And that little boy?" she retorted.

"I know," he said. "But there were other people around. It wasn't your responsibility."

Dee knew a moment's exasperation before her eyes focused on the fine lines of strain that furrowed the faint crow's-feet on Nick's face. She remembered how frightened she'd been for him when he'd been bullfighting during the rodeo. She hadn't his training or his swiftness, and knowing that must have made the watching that much worse for him. She saw it now in his eyes, in the gentle but firm way he held her, in the light trembling of his fingers resting on her shoulders.

She clasped her hands over his. "Maybe it's about time you saw this job of yours from the other side. Fighting bulls is pretty scary stuff."

"There's a difference. I'm the trained professional."

"Yeah, you do it on purpose, and I do it when I don't have a choice," she said, backing away. "Excuse me. I'd like to wash some more of this dirt off."

Looking pensive, he dropped her hand and turned away. "Go ahead. There's a clean towel in the cabinet under the sink," he said.

While she scrubbed away the worst of the grime from the rest of her, she could hear him repacking the first-aid kit. By the time she emerged, he was bent over what passed for a kitchen sink, scrubbing his face.

He looked up as she approached, grinning ruefully. "I hadn't quite finished removing the makeup when I heard all the commotion. A quick wipe with a towel doesn't quite do the trick," he explained. "My face was starting to itch, just thinking about it. I don't know how women can stand to wear the stuff."

She chuckled, relieved that the tension between them had eased. "I don't think it's quite the same. That greasepaint's a lot heavier than anything I ever used, even in my teenage experimental period."

Nick looked thoughtful as he hesitated a moment. "Now that you mention it, I seem to remember some blue eye shadow—"

"You would," she replied with a wry smile. His answering grin had a strange effect on her equilibrium. She turned away, searching the counter for her cup, finding it immediately.

"There's more in the cabinet," he offered.

"No thanks. You'd have to carry me back to my room," she retorted, then bit her tongue at the image of her in his arms. It almost tempted her to reach for that bottle, but she didn't. She didn't want the next time in his arms to be clouded in an alcoholic fog. Assuming there *was* a next time, she thought, with a surreptitious glance his way. He held himself stiffly, moving with swift, controlled motions. He was exhausted and tense, a combination that didn't speak well for any romantic yearnings she might have.

It's just as well, she told herself. An affair with Nick

would be the height of stupidity. Rummaging around in the refrigerator, she found a jug of cold water and poured herself a cup.

"Pour some for me, too, please," he asked, then wiped at his face with a towel. By the time she handed the glass over, he'd removed almost all trace of the greasepaint.

"Missed a spot," she commented, rubbing at a red streak at his temple. The light touch turned to a caress as their eyes caught and held.

Nick clasped her hand, halting the soft stroking. This time he couldn't mask the desire that flared as he hesitated on the brink of decision. She didn't give him a chance to back away. She leaned close, brushing up against him as she touched his lips.

"Thank you for being here when I needed you."

"I didn't do anything," he replied tensely, combing his fingers distractedly through his hair. "Heck, I knew that bull was trouble. He was just looking for a way out all day. I should have insisted they double-check the fences or move him to a more secure pen. I shouldn't have been in such a damned hurry to get back here and clean up. You could have been killed, you know."

She straightened, watching his changing expressions through puzzled eyes. Fear, desire, and then finally self-castigation crossed his features in quick flashes.

"I'm fine," she reminded him. "Nobody was hurt, not really. And don't paint me as some sort of saint. I just did what anyone else would have done. It was no big deal."

He reached out, clasping both of her hands in his and pulling her so close that her knees bumped against the worn cushions of the bench. "It was incredibly brave. And if you ever do anything like that again—I couldn't watch something like that again."

Startled by his intensity, Dee studied his face as his eyes clenched closed, and he tensed all over.

"You saw it happen?" She'd thought he was only worried because she'd lost her composure, had acted like a crazy woman for a while.

He nodded, then fumbled agitatedly with her hands. "Part of it. I couldn't get there fast enough to get the boy or you out of the way. I saw you run, then the bull cut between us, and I couldn't see what happened to you. You just disappeared." His voice cracked. He blinked hard, breathing in sharply before he continued. "Now I know how it feels to watch and not be able to do a damn thing," he admitted.

His strained tone tugged at her already overwrought emotions, sending prickling tears to the corners of her eyes. But crying would be the ultimate indignity, she thought, struggling to control the feelings that threatened to break loose.

Then his lips trembled on hers in the barest of kisses. He touched her carefully, as if she would shatter beneath her fingertips. *I won't break*, she wanted to say, but didn't know how to say it without revealing how much she wanted him. Not his comfort or his compassion, but him—his arms around her, his lips on hers, his body against hers, joined with hers. It was the whiskey, she thought, combined with the effects of the old attraction she'd felt all day. It couldn't be anything more, not in the short time they'd had together, not with nothing more in common than teenage memories and a weakness for chili dogs. This intense desire was simply another form of reaction, and it would go away in a few minutes.

"I wasn't brave," she said in a whisper when he lifted his head. Slowly he eased himself back, giving her bare inches of space to breathe.

"You were," he insisted.

"Bravery requires some kind of forethought, a choice you make. I didn't think," she argued. She started to move away, but his fingers crept up her arms, softly stroking, sending tiny shivers through her entire body. Finally, he rested his hands on her shoulders and eyed her intently.

"You could have run the other way," he said, then touched his lips to hers when she started to argue again. "Don't say it. You can't change my mind, and you'll only make me angry if you try."

She started to speak, but stopped herself as she realized the tense set of his muscles revealed more than self-castigation. She cupped his cheek, then let her fingers slide down to the pulse point at the base of his jaw. She felt the racing beat there before he captured her hand and pressed a kiss to her palm.

He desired her, she knew. Why was he holding back? Why was she? His eyes darkened, the pupils expanding, deepening the warm brown to midnight blackness. His breath hissed through his teeth as she touched his chest, then slowly undid the top button.

He captured her hand, stopping her. "Dee?" His tone was half questioning, half warning. "You have no idea what you're doing to me."

She pulled her hand from his grasp and reached for the second button, then the third. "I think I do. I hope I do," she whispered, sinking into his lap.

Nick groaned softly and clutched her tightly. "You've changed a bit. You used to be shy," he whispered against her neck, spacing the words between nibbling kisses that weakened any remaining doubts that lingered in her mind.

Dee's low, soft laugh was her only answer before she shifted and met his lips with her own. This time, his mouth wasn't gentle as he taunted and teased, demanding a response that matched his need.

Desire swirled around her, through her, until she couldn't think anymore. She could only feel the heat between them, his hands on her arms, her body, the cooling breeze from the window, then the heat of his touch once again.

By feel, she located the remaining buttons, then eased them through the buttonholes and pushed his shirt aside while he did the same to hers. Then he pushed aside the thin lace of her bra to cup her small, rounded breasts, stroking with whispering touches until she felt the tugging pull of her nipples and the answering tug between her thighs.

Her hand fumbled with his belt, and he lifted his head. "You're sure?" he asked.

She met his gaze squarely, not even attempting to veil what she was feeling. Old emotions sprang anew, glimmering in their maturity, casting a warm glow over her soul. "I'm not fifteen anymore. And I know very well what I'm doing."

"Good. Because I want you."

She nodded slowly. "I can't remember wanting anything more," she replied, gazing at him through passion-clouded eyes.

Fire flashed back at her. He kissed her hard until she couldn't breathe. Then she realized she'd only forgotten to breathe. She filled her lungs with an exhilarating rush of air and flung her head back with a joyous laugh.

Nick wrapped his hands in her hair, then nibbled a path down her neck to the hollow between her breasts. Sweet lethargy seeped through her muscles. She swayed back, grasping his shoulders for support as he teased one raised nipple, then the other.

Her hands seemed to move of their own volition, tightening around his arms, then sliding lower to feel the hardness through the tight denim. She touched, caressed, with insistent fingers that knew more of what she wanted than her conscious mind. An instant later he lifted his head and pushed her gently to her feet.

"Not here," he said with a rueful glance at the cramped bench seat. "I think it would be impossible anyway."

Turning her around, he nibbled lightly at her neck, sending delicious tremors along her nerve endings to the heat building at her core. Her knees weakened and she swayed backward, leaning against the solid warmth of his chest.

"Nothing's impossible," she pointed out, reaching over her shoulders to touch him, to cup his smooth-shaven cheek in the palm of her hand. She felt the warmth of his lips on her palm and spun back into his arms.

"I'd rather not test that point tonight," he replied, gently propelling her toward the curtain at the opposite end of the trailer. As they passed, he clicked the lock on the trailer door.

"What about Matt?" she asked, halting.

Nick frowned as he considered the problem of his partner, then a slow smile crossed his lips. "He'll be gone for hours. That should be time enough."

Dee's brows tilted skeptically. "Do you think so?" Then she turned and walked down the narrow passage, unfastening her jeans as she walked. She stepped behind the curtains into the dimness beyond.

Seconds later, he joined her. "No, don't," he said, pulling her hands away from the jeans zipper. She stilled, thinking for an instant that he'd changed his mind. His fingers replaced hers, fumbling for a moment, then nimbly sliding the zipper down.

He pushed the denim over her hips toward the floor, teasing and caressing with his fingertips. He nudged her back against the wall, trapping her with the length of his body.

"Magic," he whispered, then kissed her with lingering sweetness. A depth of emotion quivered in his voice, a sense of reverence mingled with awe. Something untamed burst free inside her. She circled his waist with her arms, loving the feel of his flesh next to hers, the heat of him, the strength of him.

He lifted her onto the mattress nestled high in the gooseneck of the trailer. She kicked her ankles free of the blue jeans and lay back, listening to the soft rustling as he kicked free of his own. Then he was there beside her, touching and tasting until she thought she would go mad.

So she took her turn, reaching out tentatively at first to feel bare, taut flesh, then more boldly to learn every part of him. She teased back, answering him touch for touch, stroke for stroke. Her tongue circled one flat male nipple, then the other, and she remembered how he'd done the same to hers not a moment before. She kissed lower, and lower still, following the tickling hairs that arrowed to his waist and below.

Then in a lightning-swift move, he rolled and pinned her beneath him. A low chuckle escaped her as she danced her fingers up his spine, then back. Magic, he'd said. She felt it, too, though even now she hadn't the courage to say so. It was enough to just feel it, to touch and be touched.

Her mind couldn't comprehend these feelings, so she quit trying and let instinct take control. She pressed against him, feeling the insistent throb in return. Then finally, he parted her legs and slipped between her thighs. He moved with maddening slowness, still teasing her, teasing them both, until she began to shudder.

She gasped for air, clenching the hard-muscled shoulders as she felt a thousand tiny explosions. After that there was only pleasure, mindless, satiating pleasure that lifted and swelled in the blackness of the night. It was like nothing she'd ever known or imagined. For an instant she tasted heaven and knew that she never wanted to leave it.

It was a long time before either of them spoke. At first she thought he'd drifted off to sleep. David had always fallen asleep once his needs had been satisfied, but somehow she'd expected Nick to be different. He was, she reminded herself, thinking of the spiraling passion and the shattering culmination of their lovemaking. Just thinking of it warmed the smoldering ashes.

Then he moved beside her, stroking that desire to a peak that was even higher than before. And when it was over, they lay entwined in peaceful silence.

"That was amazing," she whispered.

"*You're* amazing," he replied. "I always knew you would be."

Dee stilled, digesting that. His words implied a timelessness, a sense of history she'd never considered. He sounded as if he'd thought of her in these terms before, but she knew that couldn't be true. She'd been a pest, a *menace*, to use his own words.

He pulled her close. He wanted to hold her close, to pretend for a while that they would be this way again and again. He regretted that it had taken so long for him to discover how she felt against him. He was grateful for this one chance. Still, he couldn't help but resent the years between the imagining and the reality.

"Tell me about your marriage," Nick whispered in the darkness.

"Why? It has nothing to do with you and me. It was over years ago, almost before it began," she replied.

He felt her shift in the darkness, snuggling into the crook of his arm. "Craig called him a Peter Pan," he prompted.

"He was," she answered. "Still is, by all accounts."

Nick stiffened. "You've kept in touch?"

She twisted around in his arms and pressed a kiss to his chest. "I still hear about him through friends. And we have the same agent."

"He's an artist, too?" Nick felt the chasm between them widen again.

"A sculptor. He's good, but it's not much of a living."

Nick understood more from what she didn't say than what she did. "You supported him, didn't you? And he resented your success?"

He felt her shrug. "Maybe. I'm not sure. That's not why we divorced."

"Then why?"

"We had different definitions of fidelity," she replied. "David's living in Italy now, soaking up inspiration from the ruins and the crumbling statues. And if I know him, he has plenty of accommodating companionship."

"How could you marry someone like that?" Nick said, then instantly regretted it. "Sorry. It's none of my business."

"You're right. But since you're curious enough to ask," she continued, "I thought I loved him. I thought we had a lot in common. We did, but not the right things. Now can we talk about something else?"

"What?"

"Tell me about the ranch. Tell me what's changed and what's the same."

"Do you really care? Or are you just trying to change the subject?"

"Both," Dee replied. "Sometimes I remember the sunsets over the hill or the night sounds. Are there still coyotes in the hills?"

They talked long into the night, or rather Nick talked. He told her about the new pond, about the herding dogs and the cantankerous stallion who'd been a yearling the year she'd left. He told her about everything and nothing—details she could see in her mind, but nothing of the vague sense of dissatisfaction all the work couldn't erase.

Long after her breathing evened out in sleep, he lay awake savoring the closeness and wondering how he would find the courage to let her go in the morning.

NINE

The sun streamed through the tall, second-story windows of Dee's studio, throwing warm light across the half-finished sketch on the drawing board. Dee lifted her brush and sighed, wishing she'd never let Craig's enthusiasm lure her into this project. If she hadn't, she wouldn't have met Nick again. She was beginning to believe that would have been a blessing.

She'd been back for two weeks, and she hadn't heard a word from him. She told herself once more that she shouldn't care. She hadn't asked for promises and he hadn't given any. She didn't even know how she felt about the night they spent together, not in the larger context. She only knew that her body ached in the darkness, that she awoke hugging her pillow to her chest. Her dreams didn't bear thinking about, not if she intended to get any real work done this afternoon.

"Brooding again, darling?"

Dee glanced up, startled out of her thoughts by Pam's voice. Her mother hovered tentatively at the doorway, a worried frown highlighting the tiny lines of age showing through the finely contoured makeup.

"Just thinking, that's all. I'm having trouble with

this sketch. I can't get the hindquarters right on this calf," she explained as Pam's heels clicked on the bare wood floor.

"Work on something else for a while," her mother suggested, laying a hand on Dee's shoulder and massaging the tense knot accrued from hours bent over the sketch pad.

Dee groaned in appreciation, then rolled the shoulder, flexing the tight muscles. "Maybe you're right, Mom."

"What's this?" Dee winced as her mother spotted the Ramsey Ranch stationery and picked up the envelope. "I didn't know you'd been corresponding with Tony. Or is it Nick?"

"I haven't been exactly," Dee responded reluctantly, then spun around on her stool to face the older woman. "Nick was at the rodeo in Benton. I spent some time with him, and I promised I'd send him some photos I took. Since Nick's still on the road, Tony wrote back to thank me."

A comprehending smile crossed Pam's lips and she tilted her head toward the three sketches of Nick tacked on the wall above the drawing board. "I guess that explains those. I thought I recognized him, but it's hard to tell after ten years. I'd wondered if maybe you were just drawing from memory."

"Tony wasn't there," Dee added, watching her mother calmly. They'd never talked about the divorce, but for months afterward the woman had worn a taut, drawn look.

"I suppose he's too old for that sort of thing," Pam commented. "What's Nick up to these days?"

Dee felt herself flush, a fact that didn't slip past her mother's narrowed gaze. Stalling, Dee glanced up at the sketches, then picked up a pencil and began shading the horse's neck in the drawing in progress. "He's pretty much the same—just older and a little more careful."

Pam chuckled. "He was too smart to keep riding bulls."

"He fights them now, Mom. He's a professional rodeo clown."

"I'm not sure I'd call that smarter," Pam commented, her tone hardening. "I'd have thought he would do more with his life."

Dee bit back her resentment at her mother's tone and forced herself to remain silent.

"I'm surprised you didn't mention seeing him earlier," Pam continued with a frown. "You used to be so close. Sometimes I worried that— Well, never mind."

"You worried about what?"

Pam sighed. "You were growing up so fast, and it was obvious that Nick adored you. I told him he was too old for you, and he seemed to understand that. I wondered, though, whether he'd be able to control his feelings and wait for you to catch up with him. After we left it didn't seem to matter. You never asked about him afterward. In fact, this is the first time you've mentioned his name since the divorce."

Dee remained silent, taking in this new revelation. "I didn't realize," she said, staring back at the sketch.

"Would it have made a difference? You never seemed to miss living in the country. You were so caught up in your new school, then college, and then there was David."

Dee scowled. She had missed the farm. Daddy had seen it, and had taken her for long hikes on weekends and camping trips on summer vacations. That was how she filled her need for open space, for night sounds of crickets, whippoorwills, and distant coyotes howling. She couldn't blame Pam for not noticing how much her daughter missed certain aspects of living in the country. She'd had her own problems.

Still complete opposites, they'd grown closer after Daddy's death. It wasn't until then that Dee realized how deeply her parents had cared for each other, despite the fact they couldn't live together.

"Were you on your way out?" Dee asked.

"After a while. I forgot to tell you that Craig called earlier. He said he'd drop by to look at whatever you have ready."

Dee groaned. "Not again."

Pam smiled understandingly. "I know. He's getting to be a bit of a pest. Do you want me to talk to him when we go out tonight?"

"No, I can handle him."

Pam winked. "You're not my daughter for nothing," she quipped, then dropped a kiss on Dee's cheek. She hesitated for an instant, surveying the row of sketches of Nick. She smiled distractedly and left the room.

Dee stared at the empty doorway for a moment, wondering how much her mother suspected. Once again, she let her thoughts drift back to that last morning in Benton. They'd said good-bye in the early-dawn hours outside Dee's motel room, whispering like a couple of teenagers on the front porch. Then he'd captured her lips in one last, desperate kiss that curled her toes with passion—he'd kissed her like it was the last time.

"Promise me one thing," he'd said.

Her foolish heart had skipped a beat in the split-second pause before he'd finished. "What's that?" she'd prompted, while her fingers played with the buttons of his shirt. She couldn't meet his eyes for fear of what she'd see—or not see—reflected there.

"Smile when you think of me," he'd said.

"I'm smiling now." She stood on tiptoe to press a

kiss to each cheek, then let her fingers trail from his shoulders to his wrists.

She'd glimpsed a deep yearning before he shuttered his expression and turned away. It wasn't until after he was gone that she realized he didn't have her phone number or her address. He'd never asked for them.

With a grimace, Dee forced her attention back to her work. Several hours later, she heard Craig's crepe-soled shoes swish across the floor behind her. Figuring the cleaning lady had let him in, she gritted her teeth in annoyance. Craig and his well-intentioned suggestions right now.

"Looks great," Craig said, peering over her shoulder.

"You're kidding!" Dee glanced up in astonishment, then narrowed her gaze with suspicion. "You've picked apart everything I've drawn for the last two weeks. Did Mom say something to you after all? I told her not to."

Craig shook his head sadly, wearing a wounded look. "Am I that difficult to work with?"

Dee hesitated, thinking back over other projects she'd shared with Craig. His suggestions, his perfectionism hadn't bothered her unduly then, and he was behaving no differently than before. She was the one who had changed.

"No, I'm the difficult one," Dee apologized. "I've just been a bit off kilter since we got back."

"He hasn't called," Craig surmised.

"He won't," Dee replied. She was more sure of that than of the setting sun in her west window.

"Then you might have to make the first move," Craig said. "If you think he's worth it."

Dee didn't answer, but the thought stayed with her long after Craig and Pam had left the house. Oddly enough, it galvanized her instead of feeding the lethargy that had affected her the last two weeks. Setting aside the rough sketches, she began work in earnest on the illustrations for the bullfighting chapter. When they were finished, she'd track Nick down and use the illustrations as a pretext for seeing him.

It was nearly midnight when the jangling of the telephone startled her. She'd decided to let the machine pick it up, then changed her mind, thinking Pam and Craig might have had car trouble or some other mishap.

Nick's low voice in her ear shocked her speechless. "Dee? Is that you?"

"Y-yes," she answered in a thready voice. Emotion jolted through her, tightening her throat.

"I've missed you," he admitted. "I want to see you again."

Dee drew a deep breath. "Why now?"

He hesitated. "I can't stop thinking about that night. About you."

"I haven't forgotten, either," she admitted. "What did you have in mind."

His next words surprised her. "I'll be passing through Kansas City later this week on the way to a rodeo in Iowa. Can you come with me?"

Passing through. The words stuck in her mind, ranking right up there with one-night stand, which was all they had so far. She wanted more, though she hadn't a clue how to capture something so elusive.

"When?" she asked, stalling for time while she considered.

"Thursday night through Saturday night. I can give you a ride back to Kansas City before I have to cut over toward Columbia."

"Won't that be out of your way?"

"I want to see you. We'll have more time if we ride in the same vehicle," he reasoned. "More time to talk privately. There's too much I don't know about you."

Dee warmed at the thought. He wanted more, too.

She didn't know what was possible for them, but she intended to give herself every chance to find out. He'd unexpectedly made the first move.

"I'll be ready," she replied. "Where should I meet you?"

"I want to see where you live."

"Melody Elaine Williams!"

"What?" Dee replied, still concentrating on the half-finished watercolor in front of her. She'd been working on it since dawn, when her restlessness had driven her from her bed to her studio.

"Were you expecting someone?" Pam stood silhouetted in the doorway, an odd expression on her face. The terry-cloth bathrobe was cinched tightly at the waist, and her hair was only half combed, smooth on one side and an odd mixture of spikes and tangled mats on the other.

Dee frowned, then brushed a hand distractedly across her face. "Not this morning. Why do you ask?" *And why now?* She leaned back and squinted at the easel, then dipped her brush into the brown again.

"You didn't invite Nick Ramsey to the house?" A note of irritation entered Pam's voice. "Fine. Then I'll tell him to get lost. Unless you want to."

"Nick? He's here now?" The paintbrush clattered to the floor, splattering her bare feet and legs with chocolate speckles. "You're kidding? He's not supposed to be here until this afternoon."

Pam's tone was mildly disapproving when she answered. "Then you did expect him. Why didn't you say something? Warn me at least. I answered the door in my bathrobe, for heaven's sake. I thought it was the cleaning lady."

Dee glanced at the screen-worked clock on the wall and gasped. It was only half past seven. "Damn," she muttered, glancing around her as a sense of panic took hold. "Mother, keep him busy for a while. I have to change clothes, and I wanted to show him some of the illustrations, but I can't let him come in here until I do something with this mess—and change clothes."

"Why not? I answered the door like this," Pam pointed out, gesturing toward her makeup-free face and wildly disarrayed hair. "Why shouldn't you wallow in a little embarrassment. Share the fun."

Dee scrubbed vigorously at the paint streaks on the floor, ignoring her mother's sarcasm. "I'm sorry, Mother. You weren't around when he called. And later, I guess I just got distracted and forgot to mention it. He's waiting downstairs?"

Pam nodded and snatched the rag from Dee's hand. "Oh, go on. I'll take care of this. You're only making it worse. I can't imagine why your father put wood floors in here when tile or linoleum would have been so much more practical. Look, it's leaving a dull spot."

Dee watched her mother's bobbing head as she rubbed at the spot of paint, then dipped the rag in water to dilute the pigment. Sighing, Dee shook her head and made her escape before the situation got any worse.

Five minutes later, she stood in the hall, two steps from the living-room doorway. She'd changed her rumpled and stained tank top and cutoffs for clean jeans and a light, cotton blouse. But she didn't feel any more prepared to walk through that doorway. She didn't know what to expect. Suppose he'd changed his mind, that he'd just dropped by to disinvite her. Then she told herself she was being silly. He could have done that with a simple phone call. Or he could have simply not shown up at all. Instead he'd arrived before Pam left the house, leaving Dee with a score of awkward questions that would have to be answered sooner or later.

"What are you doing?" Pam's words hissed through the dead silence of the hallway, startling Dee.

"Checking to see whether my socks match," Dee retorted, spinning the words off the tip of her tongue. "What do you think I'm doing?"

"Stalling," Pam said loudly, then breezed past her daughter into the room.

As she passed, Dee noticed she'd smoothed down the other side of her hair, so she looked more like a quiet housewife than the Dr. Jekyll-Mrs. Hyde picture she'd presented earlier. Neither was close to the truth, but Dee kept that thought to herself. Nick seemed taken in. Of course, he'd only known Pam during her housewife mode, when she was trying to fit into the role of a good farm wife. Dee realized then that Pam hadn't hated the place, just the role she'd been playing. She was no more cut out for canning vegetables and scrubbing floors than Dee was.

"I'm just getting ready to make some coffee. Why don't you come along to the kitchen and have some whenever you're ready," her mother was saying when Dee crossed the threshold. Anything after that was lost as Dee absorbed the sight of the man she'd dreamed about these past two weeks.

The reality outweighed anything she'd remembered, and her sketches didn't do him justice, either. In the flesh, Nick Ramsey was too arrestingly alive for words. Nothing could encapsulate the intangible quality that set him apart from other people—not paint, not letters strung together. Dee could only feel him reaching out to enfold her in his spell.

"I guess I should have called," he said, without a hint of apology. "But I was afraid you'd change your mind and wouldn't be here if I waited until this afternoon."

The dark shadows beneath his eyes and the drawn

lines around his mouth hinted at fatigue, but he rose from the sofa and moved toward her with tightly leashed energy in each step. Pam backed out of the room, murmuring something about croissants and coffee.

"Are we alone yet?" he whispered after a moment.

"Yes." The word had barely left her mouth when his arms closed around her, crushing her against his chest. Then his lips met hers in a frantic kiss that fed on the memory of doubts, fears, and long days apart.

"I missed you," Dee whispered, when they drew a scant inch apart.

"Me, too," he replied. "I couldn't sleep last night. So I got in the truck and drove."

"The horses?"

"Matt has them. I have the camper," he replied.

Dee chuckled. "Did you park out front?"

"I could move it," he offered.

"Not a chance. It'll give the neighbors something new to talk about," she replied.

He trailed kisses up her neck, stopping close to her ear. "Maybe I should hang Matt's favorite prop in the window."

Dee let her head sag back as the sensuous feel of his lips on her flesh stole her thoughts. "What's that?" she asked distractedly. His fingers slipped beneath the back of her blouse, trailing tantalizing paths of fire up her spine until they reached her bra clasp.

"Let me give you a hint," he whispered.

"Yes?" When he didn't answer, she leaned back, studying his expression. Mischief danced in his eyes, and she had a quick mental picture of hot pink and lace.

"Forget it," she replied. "They don't need that much to talk about." Then her arms circled his neck, pulling his lips closer to hers again.

"Your mother?" he asked.

"You're right," Dee replied, pulling away. "One shock before breakfast is enough."

"How much have you told her?" He laced his fingers through hers, keeping her close with the subtle pressure of the movement while his thumbs drew tingling circles on her wrists.

"Only that you were in Benton," she answered, swaying toward him. His eyes were unreadable, hiding his thoughts from her. As his thumbs stilled on her pulse point, she sensed a subtle change in him.

"I've wondered whether you'd said anything."

"I had to. She found the note from Tony." At his puzzled look, she explained about the prints she'd sent to the farm and about Tony's reply.

"And that's all you told her?" he asked when she was finished. His displeasure flashed across his face as he released her hands and turned away, running his fingers through his sand-colored curls. "What about Craig?"

"What about him?" Dee replied with exasperation. "Do you really think he came back and said, 'Pam, darling. Your daughter nearly got stomped by a bull, but it's all right now. And by the way, she didn't come back to her room that night because she was shacked up with your ex-stepson.' Craig's a little strange sometimes, but he's not stupid."

Nick spun around, his mouth opened to speak when his gaze focused somewhere behind her. "Mrs. Williams—er, Ramsey," he squeezed out in a strangled voice.

"Just call me Pam. It's simpler," the woman said.

"Mom, I—"

Pam tilted her head and held up a staying hand. "I just came to tell you the coffee's ready. Anything else can wait until the two of you make sense of it. Somehow I think I'll be less confused that way,'' she said with a firm shake of her head. "Now, I have to get ready to go into the office."

Dee listened to her mother's soft footfalls as she crossed the hall and took the stairs to the second floor. Then she felt Nick's hands on her shoulders.

"Do you intend to go to Iowa with me?" he demanded in a deceptively soft voice.

"Of course," she said. "If you still want me to."

He dropped a light kiss on her forehead. "Then let's have some of that coffee."

"Sure," she replied, taking his hand and leading him across the vaulted entry and down the wide hallway to the kitchen. The sunny, cozy room was a sharp contrast from the white, airiness of the rest of the house. Although the windows were tall here, too, the richly grained cabinets and yellow-flowered wallpaper were more welcoming than the high, stark walls and dramatic ceilings of the other rooms.

"Nice," he commented, his eyes widening with surprise. "Are you sure we're in the same house?"

Dee nodded. "Mom and I did this room over when we moved in. The rest is pretty much the way Dad left it. Dad never could do kitchens. He put white carpeting in here." She poured out two cups of coffee and handed one to Nick. "It's decaf," she warned. "And a bit on the thin side." She didn't think so, though she knew he would.

He sipped it with a neutral expression. "It's fine."

"Have you had breakfast yet?"

"I drove straight through. I thought maybe we could go out."

"Let's not," she replied, pulling open the refrigerator and rummaging around. "Let's see. We have eggs, bacon, leftover spaghetti sauce and two eggrolls, mushrooms, cheese. How about an omelet?"

"Sounds interesting."

Dee glanced over the top of the refrigerator door and grinned. "Just how interesting would you like it?" she teased.

His smile faded as the smoldering flashed through his eyes, followed by a burning look that riveted her to the spot, unmindful of the cold air billowing out of the refrigerator. "We're not alone yet," he reminded her. "If we were, I'd make you pay for that one, and I don't think you'd mind a bit."

Dee's mouth went dry, all thoughts of breakfast forgotten in a rising haze of passion. He could stir her with a word, a look. It wouldn't matter what she was doing or who she was with. He could make her forget everything but how she felt when he touched her.

Forcing herself to look away, Dee turned back to the refrigerator and withdrew several containers. "Let's worry about food first," she said, striving for a flip tone. Then she realized the implication of what she'd said. Food first, and then? His languorous smile told her he'd caught the double entendre as well, and she sent him a quelling look.

"Cheddar or Monterey Jack?" she asked in as stern a voice as she could manage.

"For what?"

"The omelet, you idiot. Never mind, you can eat what I give you."

"Anytime," he said, slipping up behind her. His warm breath at her ear sent shivers down her spine. Her grip slackened on the egg carton in her hand, and it crashed to the floor.

"Damn," she said, pulling away and grabbing for a dishtowel.

He beat her to it and hastily began to sop up the broken eggs with one hand while he gathered up shells in the other. "Good thing the white carpeting's gone," he commented. "What's that on your foot?" He mopped away a streak of egg with a dry corner of the towel, with soft strokes that only fed the heat fanning out from her midsection.

Dee stared down at the top of his head and clenched her hands into fists to keep from tangling them in the short, sandy curls. "Nick?" she began in a strangled voice.

"What?" He touched her ankle, and she jerked it away.

"Nick, go in the other room. I'll take care of this."

"I'll get it," he insisted. "It's my fault. I shouldn't have teased you like that."

"Get out of the kitchen. Now," she repeated, her tone firming with each syllable. "I'll call you when breakfast is ready."

He hesitated, then nodded and pushed himself to his feet. "You're right. I'll be in the living room," he said. Then he disappeared around the corner, whistling a jaunty tune.

"Had to have the last word, didn't he?" Pam commented from the doorway when he was gone.

"How long have you been standing there?"

"Long enough," she said, glancing at her watch. "I have to run now or I'll be late for my first appointment. Will you be home when I get back this evening?"

Dee lifted her chin. "No. I'm going to a rodeo with Nick."

Pam stared at her daughter thoughtfully. "Then I'll just say this for now. Enjoy it while it lasts, but don't lose your head. The Ramsey men can be very charming and damned persuasive. And while you're at it, don't forget what happened with David."

Dee felt a surge of anger that her mother could compare Nick with David, a self-centered child in a man's body. "Just come right out and say it so I won't misunderstand you, Mother."

Pam caught Dee's hands in her own. "You're too much like me," she said. "We really have no judgment about men. So have an affair if you must. Go away for the weekend, and another, and another until you work these feelings through. But don't let yourself be taken in by them. And don't make the same mistake you made with David. Don't trust him with your heart."

Pam's brows were knit in a worried frown, deepening the furrows across her forehead. Dee didn't know how to answer her. She'd harbored some of the same doubts herself. Yet Nick was not like David; she was sure of that. In his own way, Nick had always been there to help her when they'd both lived at the farm. And he cared for her, the woman she'd become as well as the child she'd been. David had cared only for himself. She'd just been too blindly in love to see it. This time, she had her eyes open.

"Mom, I have to do this," Dee replied in a voice so calm and firm it surprised even her. "I can't go through the rest of my life wondering. I just have to trust my instincts. I have a lot of Daddy in me, too, and he had pretty good instincts."

Pam gave a noncommittal shrug. "Maybe. Just be careful. And let me know before you do anything foolish. At least give me an opportunity to talk you out of it."

Dee chuckled. "As if I'm going to recognize stupidity at the time."

"I know, I know. Now I have to run. You'll be back on Sunday?"

"I think so," Dee said. When her mother hesitated at the doorway, Dee sighed. "It's just a figure of speech. Of course I'll be back. I'm not about to abandon Craig in the middle of this book, not to mention a couple of other projects sitting upstairs. Now get going, before you're late."

It wasn't until she heard the front door click closed, however, that she turned her attention back to the mess on the floor. She carefully retrieved the three eggs that had survived the fall, then mopped up the rest. And she wondered which category she'd fall into over the next few weeks, the survivors or the crushed.

No, she told herself. She didn't have to be either. There was a third alternative, one she hadn't let herself consider before now. She might find a place where she belonged. Considering the thought, she quickly prepared a simple omelet, then called to Nick.

When he didn't answer, she set the food on the warming tray and went in search of him. She figured he'd either gone out to the truck to get something or had wandered elsewhere in the house. There were enough unique paintings and odd pieces of pottery, sculptures, and quaint furniture to lead anyone with an ounce of curiosity from room to room.

She found him in a corner of the living room, stretched out in the oversized lounge chair she hadn't found the courage to dispose of yet. Daddy's chair.

"Nick? Breakfast is ready," she said softly as she gave his arm a gentle nudge. When he didn't answer, she drew back and watched him for a moment. Now that he was asleep, she could see the signs of exhaustion more clearly, and she felt a pang of guilt that she was the cause. He'd driven straight through, probably most of the night, just to see her. He must feel the same urgency, the same confusing emotions that had disrupted her life since she'd seen him that first night in Benton. She only wished she knew where it would lead.

As quietly as she could, she tiptoed out of the room and pulled the pocket doors closed. And when the cleaning lady arrived, Dee set her to work upstairs where the noise wouldn't disturb him.

The first thing Nick saw when he opened his eyes was a boot propped against a nearby chair leg. His boot. The next thing he saw was his big toe sticking out of a hole in his sock. She'd taken his boots off without him even knowing it.

Funny, he didn't remember feeling tired, just incredibly turned on and frustrated that he couldn't, didn't dare do anything about it with Pam in the house. Not to mention the fact that Dee might have her own reservations. Seducing her after a close brush with a bull was one thing. In the bright light of day with all her defenses in place was quite another. Except he didn't recall seducing her so much as reacting to the feel of her in his arms, to the immense relief of having her safe.

She was still his Dee. He'd known that the minute she'd started to tremble with reaction, and he'd been lost. He still was. Underneath the silk and polish, she was still the same warm, caring girl she'd always been. Only the girl had grown into a woman with a body that would tempt Saint Peter himself. Just the thought of it left his mouth dry and his own body hard with wanting.

Sitting up, he reached for his boots and started to pull them on. Then one of the doors slid open to reveal a round, lined faced surrounded by a frizz of gray hair.

"Oh, my goodness, I'm sorry. Did I wake you?"

"No. Although it was about time something woke me," he said with a faint smile. Judging from the woman's dusty overalls and plastic tote tray, she was the cleaning lady Pam had been expecting when she'd opened the door to him. The look on her face had been priceless, worth the trip alone. He couldn't ever remember catching Pamela off guard in the three years she and his dad were married. She'd been almost too perfect, too controlled to be real.

He glanced at his watch and groaned. Two o'clock. Unbelievable. Tugging his boots on the rest of the way, he watched the woman as she worked around the room with a dusting rag.

"Is Dee still here?"

"Miss Williams?" the woman asked without a break in motion. "She's in her studio."

"Where's that?"

"Oh," the woman said, staring at him nonplussed. "I just assumed you knew. You were sleeping there so comfortably, and Miss Williams said . . . Oh, never mind. It's none of my business. My tongue's always getting me in trouble anyway."

His boots now back on, he leaned back in the chair. "What did Miss Williams say?"

"Well, if you insist. She told me to feed the leftovers in the kitchen to the neighbor's dog. She said you'd fallen asleep before your omelet was ready." A disapproving frown creased the woman's face as she applied extra pressure to the tabletop she was buffing.

Mindful of Dee's reputation in the neighborhood, he choked back the rumble of laughter that threatened. "I drove all night to get here," he explained. "I believe the neighbors across the street can confirm my arrival time. They waved from the front porch."

"That would be the Jacobsons. I do their place on Fridays," she confirmed.

Mission accomplished, he thought as he left the room. He still didn't know where Dee's studio was, but he wasn't about to ask the self-righteous biddy again. Detouring to the kitchen, he grabbed an apple from a fruit basket on the counter, then strolled through the house while he ate it.

He recognized a few photographs and the stained-glass curio cabinet in the dining room. The only other clues to Dee's existence were three paintings, all signed by her. All were outdoor scenes, close-detailed pictures of something that obviously intrigued her, with a big background of slightly vague vistas. One was a sweet william growing in the edge of the woods, with an open field and deer grazing beyond it. Another was of an old foundation, with the crumbled remains of a house lying around it. The third was a plant on a windowsill, and beyond it was the view from Dee's old room at the farm.

Nick felt like he'd been punched in the stomach, the emotion hit him so hard. She remembered every detail, and cared enough to hang the painting in her home where she'd see it every day. Yet she'd been less than happy to see him two weeks ago, and her reasons didn't stop with the prank he and Matt had played on her. He knew a deep pain as he realized it wasn't the farm she'd wanted to forget. It had been him. He'd brought it on himself. He'd hurt her when he was only trying to save her and himself from his overactive libido.

He mounted the stairs quickly, ignoring the painting on the landing. She wasn't downstairs, so she had to be up there. He stopped at the first door and decided the neatly made bed and ruffled curtains couldn't belong to Dee.

The one across the hall was more like her, with unassuming curtains and furnishings that didn't compete with the art on the walls or the clutter of strange carvings and statuettes scattered around the room. It was a museum of sorts, but not a workplace.

He found her, finally, in a large sunny room at the far end of the hall. Bending over the tilted table, she seemed a different person. He watched for a moment as the fleeting emotion crossed her face—deep concentration, dissatisfaction—then a few pencil strokes later, a faint glimmer of excitement and something else. Was it love, or had he imagined the brief play of her features before her brows drew back together in concentration?

Then she noticed him, and the elusive emotion played across her features again, warming him more than the sun at first light.

"What are you working on?" he asked.

"Nothing much." She shrugged, shuffling the papers. "Do you want to see some of the illustrations for the book? I have a few finished, and sketches for several others."

"I'd love to," he said, moving closer.

"I see you found your boots," she commented as his heels sounded loudly on the bare floor. She didn't mention the condition of his socks, but the glimmer in her eyes told him she remembered. He counted himself lucky she hadn't painted the offending toenail shocking pink.

Then he turned his attention to the sketch she held up. It was good, better than he'd expected, and he'd expected a great deal after finding those paintings downstairs. "You've caught the flex of the muscles really well," Nick said as he examined a painting of a bull rider coming out of the chute. "Not just on the animals, but on the riders, too. You can almost see this guy's arm pulling at the socket when the bull jerks."

Dee shrugged, though there was pride in her expression. "I studied anatomy in college, and last week when I was having trouble with the bull's hindquarters I looked up some veterinary texts at the library."

Nick nodded, impressed. Then he noticed the painting on the facing wall, next to the door. "That building looks familiar. I think I've seen it before."

"You may have. It's the Oakston Building in Tulsa. Daddy designed it."

"And you painted it? Why?" Nick was intrigued. It

wasn't anything like her other paintings. The colors were stark, muted browns and grays, the city in winter. The building rose from the ground like a monolith and was reflected in a large pool. A black-haired child with a purple teddy bear stood next to the pool, feeding the geese.

"Daddy painted it, most of it at least. I finished it after he died," she explained.

"That doesn't tell me why?"

"I did it because it needed to be finished. And I felt better when it was done. As for Daddy, I guess it was sort of symbolic," she said, stepping closer and staring at the painting with a secretive smile. "The little girl is me, and the Oakston Building was his biggest triumph after he left the firm and struck out on his own. It's the building he'd been wanting to do for years."

Nick was silent for a moment, digesting her words. "Why do you hang it here?" he asked.

Dee hesitated. "Promise you won't laugh."

"Why would I?"

"It's kind of silly."

Nick dropped an arm around her shoulder and pulled her close. "Have I ever laughed at something that was really important?"

Dee smiled up at him, warming him with the trust in her eyes. "It's a reminder of who I've been and what a person can be. When I'm working on some company calender illustration or an ad for laundry detergent, I can look up there and think about what it takes to make wishes come true. It's enough to make me stick with the work at hand so I can finish it, pay the bills, and then do something fun."

"And where does Craig's book fit in?"

Dee shrugged. "It's better than laundry detergent. I like the idea of entertaining kids and helping them understand something new. But I still have to meet a deadline, no matter how much I'd rather be doing something else or how rotten I feel when I get up in the morning. It's still someone else's concept and someone else calls the shots. And they're very specific about what they want."

Nick couldn't help the grin splitting his face. He hadn't realized the parallels in their lives before. On the surface, they seemed so very different. But he was discovering more common threads with each hour. She didn't realize it, but she'd just spouted his basic life philosophy. He kept on clowning, even when he hurt, because he could make a difference—and because the money made a difference. He'd been able to put the farm back in the black, thanks to his rodeo work. And that was no small feat.

The gulf between him and Dee had narrowed in his mind, and he began to hope for more than a few scattered weekends together.

TEN

Dee rubbed her hands across her bare arms and glanced again at the thunderheads rolling in from the southwest. She'd dressed for the muggy heat of that afternoon, but an early-evening shower had brought a cold front. The forecast for central Iowa predicted more of the same. However, neither the rodeo sponsors nor the participants seemed too concerned about the dropping temperature or the brisk breeze that had sprung up. Only a hailstorm or a tornado would stop tonight's performance.

"I think I'll go get a jacket," she told Nick, excusing herself from the group clustered around the announcer's booth. "Do you want anything? A sandwich or something to drink."

He shook his head and added a wink that lent a provocative note to his next words. "I'll have something later."

Dee's only reply was an impudent wink of her own, before she ambled away with a bit more swing to her step than usual. Back at the trailer, she exchanged the thin eyelet blouse and shorts for a more sensible cotton shirt and jeans. She was still debating about the jacket when the door opened.

"Change your mind?" she asked as she turned, then bit back her next words. She didn't know who was more surprised, herself or the woman framed by the open doorway.

"Sorry. I didn't know you were in here," the woman said, looking faintly embarrassed. Then her eyes narrowed with suspicion. "Who are you?"

Dee struggled with the faint sense of familiarity at the woman's slightly husky voice, but she couldn't place her.

"Are you here with one of the guys or are you looking for spare cash?" the woman continued. Her possessive tone raised Dee's hackles, but she covered her irritation with a composed smile.

"I'm here for the weekend. My name's Melody Williams, but most people just call me Dee."

If anything, the woman's demeanor cooled even more as she stepped the rest of the way inside and closed the door. "I'm Freda Millikan, a close friend."

"That's it," Dee exclaimed. "I remember you. Barrels, right? You guys used to call yourselves the three caballeros. You have a sister named . . . Amanda, no—Mandy."

"You're right," Freda replied, still cool. "But I'm sorry. I don't remember you."

Dee shrugged. "I hope not. I was a knock-kneed kid with braces. Your sister used to tell me I'd look better once I put on a little makeup."

Recognition dawned slowly across Freda's face, followed by wide-eyed surprise. "You're *that* Dee?"

Exasperation with the woman flared, and Dee forgot about discretion.

"If you mean the Dee that used to tag around after Nick until Mom divorced Tony, yeah. I'm that Dee." Her cool smile was quickly slipping. Freda also might be one of Nick's former girlfriends. Or maybe former wasn't the accurate term, she added to herself with a faint shiver of unease. That would explain her antagonism.

Freda sank into a seat with a relieved sigh. "Thank God." A sheepish grin replaced the frown.

"Who did you expect?" Dee didn't know what to make of Freda's reaction so she simply grabbed her jacket and headed for the door.

"Don't go yet," Freda said, holding up her hands in a gesture of surrender. "Really, I'm sorry. I'm not usually this crazy. It's just that the last time I saw a strange woman in the trailer, she turned out to be Matt's new girlfriend." Her tone made the word "girlfriend" sound like an obscenity.

Dee's only answer was a subtle lift of her brows. She wouldn't touch that one with a ten-foot pole, but she suspected this Freda had more than a casual interest in Matt. Whether the interest was hopeful or the result of bitter experience, Dee couldn't tell.

"If I see Matt I'll tell him you're looking for him," she offered. "Or was it Nick you wanted to see?"

"Either," Freda replied. "I just wanted to say hello. I haven't seen them since Oklahoma City a week ago." As she spoke, she followed Dee out of the trailer and nuzzled the nose of a sleek bay mare tied nearby.

"Is she yours or borrowed?" Dee asked, noting the mare's affectionate nudge to Freda's shoulder while the woman untied the reins.

"I bought her from Nick this spring. She's young yet, but she's coming along pretty well. Next year she'll be ready to compete full-time."

"You don't use her now?" Dee thought it was a bit strange to haul a horse all over the country if you weren't going to use it. Expensive, too.

"Sometimes at smaller rodeos like this one. She's still a bit flighty around crowds, although she's settled down quite a bit in the last couple of weeks. I use Ginger at the bigger rodeos where there's more money involved. Also, it's nice having a backup horse along, just in case,'' she added.

''I can see the sense in that,'' Dee replied, then smiled as she started to move away toward the bleachers. ''Nice meeting you again. I suppose I'll see you around the next couple of days.''

Freda grinned. ''Guaranteed. Nick always said I'm harder to get rid of than cockroaches. Come to think of it, I believe I recall him saying that about you a time or two.''

Dee rolled her eyes. ''I guess I was a pest when I was a kid.''

''He acted like you were, but he didn't have to let you hang around. He could have gotten rid of you easily enough if he'd wanted to. I've seen him do that often enough.''

''That's encouraging,'' Dee replied, then hesitated before voicing the concern that had been uppermost on her mind for the better part of the afternoon, of the week, really.

''Freda? You care about them a great deal, don't you?''

''We go way back.''

''How can you stand to watch them work? It scares the hell out of me.''

Freda's sympathetic smile said more than words. She wasn't antagonistic anymore, or condescending, as Dee had feared. She understood.

''You take a deep breath, pray a lot, and trust that they know what they're doing. And sometimes it's just easier to close your eyes,'' she said.

''That's it?''

''That's it,'' Freda repeated as she lifted her hand in

a wave. "I'd better be going. Maybe I'll see you again later."

Dee watched her go, then turned away with an amazed shake of her head. The woman was so accepting, so calm. Dee knew she couldn't ever be that way, not when the entire sport of bull riding seemed so senseless. She could see the practical applications for events such as calf roping, and even bronc riding. But what earthly reason could there be for climbing on the back of an angry bull, what reason besides the empty challenge and dangerous thrill? And without bull riders, there would be no need for bullfighting clowns.

Because it was still fairly early, she found a vacant seat in the front row close to the chutes. Ten minutes later, the entire section was filled.

While she waited for the rodeo to begin, she thought how different this one was from her working weekend with Craig. Here she sat, among strangers, with nothing to do but wait and then watch. No responsibilities. No distractions.

The thought brought a smile to her lips. She could simply enjoy the performance, most of it at least, without having to consider which angle to illustrate or how to best capture the three-dimensional, fast-paced action on a flat canvas. However, she quickly decided the facilities left a lot to be desired and wished she'd brought a cushion to soften the hard, splintery bench.

Then the opening parade of participants was launched, followed by the first heat of bull riders. Dee tensed, following Nick's every movement with fearful eyes. She had to admire how he manipulated the bull into a better performance. But did he have to get so close?

The two clowns passed close to her while they cavorted during a short break between the bull rides. Nick flashed a wide, white-toothed grin as he spotted her. A moment later, Matt nodded, too, then tipped his hat when she lifted a warning fist once again.

By the time the fourth bull emerged from the chute, she had managed to calm herself. She'd convinced herself that Nick knew what he was doing, that he'd been doing this for years without any major injuries. She just had to trust his instincts.

Then it happened. One second he was whirling and lunging, and the next he was under the beast's hooves. Someone screamed, and Dee didn't realize it was her until the woman next to her grabbed her arm. The concern on the woman's face barely registered as Dee pulled away and squeezed her way to the end of the row. She ran down the grassy aisle to the closed arena gate. She tried to push her way through, but they wouldn't let her enter. Freda appeared at her elbow, looking as pale as Dee felt.

"How bad is it?" Dee asked the man guarding the gate.

"Don't know yet."

"Let me through," Dee demanded.

"Can't." No amount of persuasion, threats, or cajoling by either of the women would budge him. It didn't matter, though, because Nick was on his feet a moment later even though he wasn't moving under his own steam. Hanging heavily on to Matt and another cowboy she didn't recognize, he limped through the gate and over to a parked ambulance. His skin was a pasty gray around the edges of the makeup Dee noticed with alarm as she reached him.

"You look terrible," she said, taking his hand. He squeezed it, then winced and tightened his hold as the paramedics ripped away his shirt. One look at the purpling hoof marks on Nick's rib cage tightened her throat with nausea.

"Let's get you to the hospital right now," she said.

She tried not to notice the hand he held stiffly to his side or the awful bleeding gash on his arm.

Then he sagged onto the stretcher the paramedics had wheeled out and grimaced. "Maybe you're right. Feels like more than a bruise this time."

This time? Dee felt the fury take hold. How many times had he been hurt? His elaborate first-aid kit was no joke, but the oozing blood brought the danger home to her. She'd nearly come to terms with it, was even beginning to relax because he always managed to scoot away without a scratch. Well, this time he hadn't, and he was damn lucky to even be alive.

By the time the paramedics had finished a rough patch job, most of the crowd had dissipated, returning to watch the rest of the rodeo. In the arena, Matt had taken over Nick's job and his barrel stood empty in the center of the arena.

"It's not as bad as it looks," Nick said. "I've had worse." Dee squeezed his hand again and dropped a kiss on his damp forehead. She didn't even want to think about this, let alone anything worse. She stepped back so the men could load the stretcher into the back of the ambulance.

"Wait," she shouted as they started to close the door. "I want to ride along." The attendant nodded and helped her inside before climbing in himself. Just before the door closed, she glimpsed Freda's concerned face and realized she'd forgotten the other woman.

The swinging doors muted the voices of the doctor and nurse working inside, but the antiseptic hospital odor managed to seep into every corner, making Dee slightly queasy. The smell overpowered even the acrid coffee that had grown cold in the styrofoam cup she held.

She glanced again at her watch and sighed, sinking

heavily into one of the ageless orange Naugahyde chairs in the corridor outside the emergency room. She'd been here two hours, and all she knew was that Nick wasn't in imminent danger of losing his life. She'd known that before they got here. He was hurt badly, but he'd been wide awake enough to argue with the ambulance driver about the relative merits of quarter horses over Morgans. So why was it taking so long for anyone to tell her anything?

She started to rise, intending to pound on the doors or push her way through to Nick. Then she caught a glimpse of the tear-streaked face across from her. The woman had arrived a few minutes after her and had silently cried ever since. Her son was behind those doors, too—a victim in a three-car pile-up, the nurse had said.

Dee sank into her chair, feeling ashamed of her impatience. The night staff of the small county hospital had enough to deal with. A ranting, complaining female would only slow them down. There was nothing she could do now to help Nick.

A moment later, Matt and Freda emerged from the front entrance.

"How is he?" Matt asked. His makeup was a bit smeared, and bits of straw clung to his jeans. They must have left the minute the rodeo ended, maybe sooner.

"I'm not sure. Nobody's told me anything. For all I know, he could still be waiting for someone to examine him," she said. "There was a big accident out on the highway right before we got here."

Freda nodded. "So that's why the ambulance never made it back to the rodeo grounds. Wouldn't they let you wait with him?"

"I did until they took him to X-ray. After that, they

brought in the accident victims and wouldn't let me back inside."

Matt sank into a chair, apparently calmer after her explanation. "That's to be expected in a place this small. They probably don't have a whole lot of space in there.

Dee drew a deep breath and settled back in her chair to wait some more. However, she was saved from further speculation or questions by the opening of the emergency room doors. Two women in shapeless blue hospital garb wheeled out a bed, and a clean-faced Nick called out a cheerful greeting.

"You three look like somebody died," Nick said. "It was just a little kick in the ribs, for Chrissake." He started to sit up, then winced and grunted.

One of the nurses frowned. "Do I have to strap you down again?"

Nick's schoolboy grin tugged at Dee's already heightened emotions. "No, ma'am," he replied. "Just give me a couple more of those pills and I'll be on my way."

"You're not going anywhere for a few days," she replied. "Doctor's orders."

Nick told her in explicit, obscene terms what the doctor could do with his orders. "I'm not staying here. This is a place for sick people," he insisted. Ignoring the woman's protests, he forced himself upright and swung his legs off the gurney.

All the blood drained from his face. But when the nurse tried to push him back down, he grabbed her wrist. "I'm leaving tonight. Now get whatever I need to sign and whatever pills the doctor prescribed so I can get out of here."

"Nick!" Dee exclaimed.

"She's right, buddy," Matt interjected. "You don't look so good right now."

Nick sneered. "Coming from a pasty-faced clown, that's real encouraging. Now get me my pants."

"You're wearing them," Matt pointed out.

Nick glanced down, then smiled grimly. "Right." He eased himself down to the floor, resting his weight on his good leg and balancing the bandaged ankle gingerly. His face was so pale, Dee feared he would pass out. She took an involuntary step forward, only to be intercepted by the nurse.

"Let's get you to your room. We'll talk about it there," the nurse insisted.

Nick hopped twice, until he reached the wall, then he shuffled his way along the wall while the nurse hurried after him.

"Forget it," Matt told her in a resigned tone. "You can't say anything to change his mind. Now just tell us exactly what's wrong with him so I can decide whose side I'm on."

Nick stopped and leaned heavily against the wall. He managed a travesty of a smile. "Three cracked ribs and a sprained ankle. That's what put me down in the first place."

"Three *broken* ribs, two cracked ribs, twelve stitches in the forearm, and an ankle that should be looked at by a specialist," the nurse recited. "You're in luck, though. Our visiting orthopedic surgeon will be in tomorrow."

"Maybe I'll get somebody to drive me back over here," Nick said, taking another hopping step.

Dee drew a deep breath and turned to the nurse. "Get the paperwork. I'll see that he signs it before we leave. Just meet us at the door."

"I'll get the car," Matt offered, leaving the two women to help Nick down the long hall to the door. Despite the nurse's arguments about hospital policy, he refused to use the wheelchair she pushed along behind him.

It took only a few minutes to produce the necessary releases, with their hastily scribbled caveats and instructions. Dee would have been surprised at the staff's speed if she wasn't so worried about Nick. By the time they piled into their borrowed car, his pallor had changed to a gray tinge.

Once inside the car, Nick's shoulders slouched. He inhaled carefully, wincing and touching a hand to the plaster cast around his rib cage. He surveyed the three of them for an instant, then growled something.

"What was that?" Matt taunted, flipping the ignition back off.

"I said . . ." Nick began, enunciating each word carefully. "This is a damned inconvenience. Hurts like hell, too."

Matt's painted smile widened, and Freda aimed a not-too-gentle punch at the man's arm. "You're a jerk," she replied before softening her tone and turning to Nick. "How long will you be out of commission?"

Nick tilted his head. "Two, maybe three weeks at the most," he estimated. "I should be okay by the end of the month."

Dee's jaw dropped in disbelief. "And in the meantime?"

"I'll haul one of the trailers, like usual. I just won't have to dress up. Actually, I might enjoy that part."

But Matt was shaking his head. "It's going to be a week before you're up to that. Maybe we can find someone to drive the truck until you're in better shape."

Nick's gaze narrowed until he stared at the three of them through slitted eyes. Then he nodded thoughtfully. "I could use a few weeks at the farm. Tony says the paperwork is really piling up. Dee, will you drive me?"

Twenty-four hours later, Dee wondered what insane notion had taken hold of her when she'd agreed. Nick wasn't a good passenger. No, that was putting it mildly. He was a horror of a passenger, and she wished she'd left him in the hospital.

She glanced over at him and sighed with relief when she saw he was still sleeping.

No, she didn't wish she'd left him. Actually, despite his bad temper, she was glad for the opportunity to spend more time with him. She only wished it was under different circumstances. Even so, she had no intention of squandering the perfect opportunity to prove she could learn again to fit into his world.

She'd discovered one thing during that long wait at the hospital and the longer night afterward while Nick slept fitfully and she slept even less. She was in love with him. Not madly, blindly in love like with David. But deeply, irrevocably in love with Nick. And she intended to do something about it.

He continued to sleep until she turned onto the dirt road that led to the farm. By the time she halted the truck in front of the house, he'd regained his bearings.

"Hasn't changed much, has it?" he said.

"Not really," she said, glancing around her. The house had a new coat of paint that was so fresh its odor still lingered in the air. They'd added a concrete sidewalk where the packed dirt path had been. Other than that, it looked the same.

She'd just unlatched her door when Nick's voice stopped her. "Dee? There's something I need to tell you about Tony. I should have said something earlier, but I've gotten so used to it that I forgot," he said.

She hesitated. "He knew I was coming, didn't he? You did call him—"

"Yes, but . . ." His voice trailed off as his eyes left her face and focused somewhere behind her.

Puzzled, she twisted in her seat and stared out the window. A wheelchair rolled around the corner, moving with frightening speed. As the chair neared the truck, it slowed and the man looked up, flashing a welcoming smile.

She felt a chill and turned pained eyes on Nick. "Why didn't anyone ever tell me?"

The man in the chair was Tony.

ELEVEN

Dee's first day back on Ramsey land was a nightmare.

She burned the omelet at breakfast, the potatoes at lunch, and the roast at dinner. The vacuum cleaner broke. The clothes dryer refused to start.

Then she'd tried to pet Nick's dog, the seventeen-year-old Australian shepherd who'd been Dog until a young Dee had dubbed her Yogi after a long-forgotten joke. Yogi bit her.

The animal was so old and weak she couldn't bite hard enough to break the skin, though. She realized her mistake immediately and apologized by laying her head against Dee's leg and drooling on her foot.

Dee scratched the dog's ears now, as she sat back against the base of the massive oak in the backyard. Nick had drifted off to sleep half an hour ago, and she'd escaped to this spot to think. She closed her eyes, letting the soft sounds of the crickets and distant barking lull her senses. Slowly, the tension eased from her body. The old dog lay her head in Dee's lap and dozed off.

None of today's mess was her fault, really. She'd

spent the day running up and down the stairs, checking on Nick, making phone calls, relaying messages, and searching out old issues of horse magazines from the basement. It was no small wonder the food was left on the heat too long.

The low hum of the wheelchair signaled Tony's approach, and she straightened, tensing again.

"Thought I'd find you here," Tony said. His voice hinted at the jovial nature she remembered. Her opinion of him inched upward. Another man might have let his condition embitter him. From what she'd seen today, Tony was the same good-natured rogue he'd always been. He just wasn't quite as mobile as before.

"This used to be my favorite spot," she said, glancing up.

She saw the subtle shift in his expression in the dying light as a hint of sadness crossed his face, followed by what looked like guilt. But that emotion didn't fit Tony.

"Did you get a chance to call your mother today?" he asked in a neutral tone.

Dee nodded. "She's bringing some of my things out next week. Nick said it would be all right, although I could just meet her in town if you don't want to see her."

His chuckle had a hard, self-accusing edge to it. "More likely she won't want to see me. Can't say I blame her, either."

Dee didn't know how to answer. Pam hadn't exactly approved of the trip to Iowa. When she learned that Dee would be at the farm for three weeks, she'd grown silent.

"She's not too pleased that I'm here," Dee admitted.

"Why are you here?" Tony asked.

Dee shrugged and started to answer in a flippant tone, but something stopped her. "Nick needed help," she said. "He couldn't drive the truck with his ribs like that, at least not for a couple of days."

Tony nodded. "And that's why you're staying for a while instead of catching the first bus out of here. So you can drive the truck until Nick is feeling better. Makes perfect sense to me," he added sarcastically. "Why don't you just come out and tell me why you're really here?"

She started to repeat her excuse about the truck, then thought better of it. It would be a waste of time to try to cover her feelings. The man had spent a lifetime watching women and charming the susceptible ones. No doubt she'd given herself away somehow.

"I'm in love with your son," she said baldly, steeling yourself for his laughter or perhaps anger.

Tony snorted. "Good grief, I know that." He sounded amused, but there was compassion in his expression.

Dee stilled. "That doesn't bother you?" she asked, watching him closely.

"Why should it?" he responded with a vague shrug. "It never did before, except that you were awfully young. I'm not surprised that the two of you picked up again where you left off."

"What are you talking about?" She rose to her feet, growing increasingly confused by Tony's attitude. "There was nothing to pick up from except a one-sided teenage crush. And I can assure you, I am not playing out some adolescent fantasy."

"Calm down, woman," Tony said, his brows drawing together in irritation. "I didn't mean to imply that. I just meant that I saw the signs years ago. You thought the sun rose and set with my boy. Your mother was afraid you'd get in over your head. I was a bit concerned myself. Nick was too young to be thinking of the consequences."

Dee bristled at Tony's criticism of his son. Nick had considered the consequences; he'd told her as much. Was that the truth, or rosy-colored hindsight? She wasn't sure it mattered whether he'd cared for her years ago or had fallen for the grown woman she'd become. He cared for her now. Maybe he was even learning to love her. The thought brought a faint smile to her lips, and she turned her head to hide it from Tony.

"I need to know if there's a future for us," she said. "If I'd finished growing up here instead of in the city, there wouldn't be any question of it, I'm sure. Eventually I would have fit in. But now I feel like I'm starting all over." She swallowed hard, then glanced up.

"What's this nonsense about fitting in? You managed well enough when you were a kid. No doubt you've learned a thing or two in the meantime that might prove useful."

"You're still a silver-tongued charmer," she said in a dry voice. "Just where did you pick up the knack of always saying the right thing?"

Tony chuckled. "You haven't changed. Don't be so suspicious. I'm on your side. I'd like to see him leave this dangerous business now that the farm is back in the black. The money helps, I'll admit, but it just isn't worth the risk. We can't keep the place going if both of us end up in these damn chairs or worse. I'd hoped he'd be smarter than me and not foul himself up."

Dee didn't know what surprised her more. His attitude or her own blunt approach. She'd intended to move slowly with Tony, to gradually get him used to the idea of having her around again. But he'd stolen her thunder.

Still, she hesitated before asking the question that had haunted her since she'd first seen him in the wheelchair.

"I know what you're thinking," he said before she could speak. "I asked for it. It's true. I'd been out with another man's wife. I dropped her off, and on the way home I wrapped the truck around a big old oak. Poetic justice, you might say,'' he added with a wink. ''However, I regret the burden my behavior put on my son's shoulders,'' he said. ''We nearly lost this place.''

''Medical bills?''

''Oh, no, no,'' he said with a rueful shake of his head. ''Insurance covered nearly everything. However, after you and Pam left, I spent too much time and money having fun.'' He said the word with a snort of distaste, tinged with regret. Then he grasped Dee's hand in a strong grip.

''Nick's spent eight years paying off the debts. He makes damn good money bullfighting. Now, he'd have to enjoy doing it some to be as good as he is. But he's put every penny back into this place, and into this horse operation he's building up. He could make a go of it now without the clowning money, but he insists he needs another year or two.

''Dee, child, he can't keep on living this way. His body won't take much more. He'll be a permanent cripple if he keeps this up.''

''I know,'' she whispered. The doctor had said as much at the hospital yesterday. He'd recommended reconstructive surgery before Nick did irreparable damage to the ankle. And it would only take one more bad fall to do it.

''Good,'' Tony said. ''I'm counting on you.'' Then he wheeled the chair back across the yard and disappeared around the corner of the house.

She stared after him, feeling slightly deflated. She'd come here, prepared to dislike the man as much as she had when she'd left. She'd been equally prepared to fight him for her place with his son. Tony made the first impossible and the second unnecessary.

* * *

By Monday, Nick was making brief trips outdoors. On Tuesday, he spent half the morning in the barn. On Wednesday, he awoke her with a slow, burning kiss before he thumped a picnic basket onto the bed beside her.

"What's this?" she asked, stretching sleepily as she struggled to shake free of the effects of the dream he'd interrupted. Already the details were fading, but she felt warm and deliciously happy.

"Breakfast and lunch. You need a break," Nick said, backing away from the bed with no more than a faint hint of the limp that had faded steadily since they'd been at the farm.

"We're going on a picnic. At this hour?" She pulled the covers back over her head and shut her eyes against the light that filtered through.

"It's half past seven, lazybones. Get up. We have to be in town by eight-thirty." The door clicked closed, then she heard him on the steps.

Sighing, she forced herself out of bed, ignoring the stiffness in her shoulders and her calves. In the past few days, she'd rediscovered muscles that hadn't been used since she was fifteen. Half a dozen times, she'd been tempted to beg Nick to massage away the soreness, but she didn't want to complain. Hard work and stiff muscles were facts of life on any farm.

Nick was whistling in the kitchen over a pan of eggs when she made her way downstairs. Turning up her nose at the grease, she set the picnic basket on the counter.

"Why don't you pack this thing while I feed the horses," she said.

"Pete can manage," Nick said, neatly flipping the eggs over. After that first day, he and Tony had resumed control of the kitchen out of self-defense. Dee had managed to spend more time outdoors, reacquainting herself with the daily tasks required for the smooth running of a horse farm.

"He's in Tucson," she reminded him. Pete's position as the farm manager had been her second surprise on the evening she arrived. After a couple of days, he'd entrusted her with a few small jobs, more to keep her busy than out of any real need for help, she suspected. Then, at Nick's suggestion, he'd gone to visit his son, leaving the two of them to manage the chores on their own for a few days.

Nick frowned as he glanced her way. "I'd forgotten. Maybe we'd better postpone the picnic. And I'll call Bob at the bank and cancel." His disappointed look reminded her that he'd been even more cooped up than she had, a condition that must be wearing for him. Besides, this business at the bank must be important, especially if it brought a banker to the office that early.

"Not a chance," she said. "Just give me a half hour or so to feed the horses and check the water troughs. I think I can still get you there on time." She snagged a couple of pieces of toast and headed out the back door.

By the time Nick reached the barn, she'd done most of the heavy work. The horses all had hay and grain mix, and the yearlings had been turned out into a nearby pasture to run. All that remained was the watering, but Dee lifted a skeptical brow when he offered to help.

"Sit," she ordered, pointing toward a scratched stool in the corner of the tack room. When that didn't work, she threatened him with a carefully directed spray of water from the hose in her hand.

"Fine, fine. I can tell when I'm not wanted." Calling to the old dog, he disappeared around the corner, but not before sending a naughty wink in Dee's direction.

She flushed, feeling the heat suffuse her. Four days

in constant contact with him had been a medley of pleasure and torture. Kisses weren't enough to satisfy the demands her body was making. On the contrary, they only made the demands more blatant. But anything more was out of the question, considering the condition of Nick's ribs. So she'd kept her distance and worked off as much of the frustration as she could outdoors—enough that she could sleep at night.

It should have taken only a few minutes to finish the chores. But while she was filling the stallion's water trough, she noticed most of his hay was on the floor. So she slipped inside the stall, talking in a low, calm voice as she caught hold of his halter and eased him back into a corner.

"Now behave yourself, Cal," she told the big black beast. He snorted and tossed his head as he nudged past her to his feed box.

It figured. Cal had been half wild as a colt. It only seemed natural that he'd prove cantankerous at middle age, she decided as she reached down to retrieve a flake of hay. But he wasn't mean or Pete would never have let her lead him out to the pasture the other day.

Thirty seconds later, she changed her mind. Cal shifted and stepped on her foot. When she leaned against him, trying to nudge him off, he leaned back at her. Her foot was in agony.

"Cal, you ugly black bag of mange, move over," she yelled, slapping at his shoulder until he sidestepped. Then he bumped against the gate. It swung wide open. The stallion smelled freedom before she could grab for his halter. He trotted through the opening and disappeared through the wide arch of daylight at the front of the barn. He was halfway across the yard, nibbling on the freshly cut lawn when she limped out of the barn.

"What happened?" Nick said, emerging from the

tack room with the drooling old dog at his heels. "I thought I heard a horse go through."

Dee sighed. She'd done it now. She'd been so intent on showing him what a good farmhand she was, she'd forgotten one of the basic rules—never leave a gate unlatched. "Cal got away from me," she answered, reaching for a lead rope. "I'd better go catch him. He doesn't still run in circles, does he?"

"Never mind that," Nick replied, running his hands up her arms. "Are you all right?" He cast worried eyes over her, settling on the mark Cal's hoof had left on her sneaker.

"I'll live," she said. "He just stepped on my foot. I'd swear he did it on purpose."

Nick chuckled and dropped a kiss on the end of her nose. "I'd better call Bob. I don't think we'll make it to town on time."

Dee felt terrible. She knew this meeting was important. Dressed in clean, creased jeans and a freshly ironed shirt and bolo tie, Nick looked ready to do business. Beside him, she felt grimy.

She *was* grimy. Cal had smeared dust and horse sweat on her, and she'd collected a few other more odorous smears on her pants legs and sneakers.

"Go on without me," she suggested. He'd driven the truck twice yesterday, claiming his ribs had healed enough to take the slight movement required for steering and shifting gears.

"Why don't you sit down over there on the bench while I catch Cal?" he retorted.

"Because I'm the one who let him get away. There's no reason for that to spoil your plans," she argued.

"Sit."

"No. I'm not your damn dog," Dee retorted. Her foot hurt like hell, and she was close to tears. But she would not cry. She grabbed the lead rope and started after Cal.

"Dee, wait!"

She kept on going.

A sharp, shrill whistle rang out. Then she heard the rattle of oats in the bottom of a bucket. Cal lifted his head and perked his ears forward. A second later, he trotted past her, burying his head in the bucket Nick held. She should have been relieved. Instead, she felt inept.

Without a word, she returned to the barn and led the horse back to his stall. Once he was inside, she secured the stall gate, then walked away, leaving the hay on the floor. Let the beast eat off of the ground—it served him right.

She walked right past the tack room without speaking. She could hear Nick on the telephone extension, talking to the banker. It only made her feel worse, and she escaped to the house before he noticed her.

Once inside the shower, she let the tears flow. When she'd finished she felt better—foolish for letting the horse get the best of her, but better nonetheless. It was one mistake, she told herself, not the end of the world or the end of her chances with Nick. So she couldn't cook when she was distracted, and she'd let his prize stallion get out. That didn't mean she hadn't also accomplished a few good things this week, like cleaning out the overgrown flower beds and feeding the horses when Pete was otherwise occupied.

She wasn't indispensable, but she wasn't a liability, either.

It took only a few minutes to slip on a clean pair of linen slacks and a silk blouse, do her hair, and add a few light touches of makeup to disguise the red puffiness around her eyes. By the time she emerged from the bathroom, she felt more like herself.

She stepped out into the hallway and ran straight into Nick's chest. "I was about ready to come in to check on you," he said, catching hold of her. "Hey, you haven't been crying, have you?"

Dee pulled away and sidestepped his embrace. "Of course not." Her tone sounded false, even to her own ears. "Let's get going. I'll get my purse and shoes, then meet you at the truck."

"How's your foot?" His tone was neutral, yet she felt the simmering frustration beneath the coolness. He was angry with her, and he had every right to be. She'd done something stupid. Nothing had happened to Cal this time, but he could just as easily have run down the driveway to the road and been hit by a passing car.

"A little sore," she answered finally. "It's nothing serious." She closed the door behind her, giving herself the privacy she needed to gather up her composure once again.

The ride into town passed in silence. Dee didn't know what to say, so she kept her mouth shut. Several times she caught his eyes on her. He seemed as uneasy as she did. She left him outside the bank, parked the truck on a side street, and went in search of a small drugstore she remembered.

It was two blocks from its old location, but it carried everything she needed. She'd only brought a weekend's supply and was running short of several necessities. Then she popped into the clothing store next door and picked out a couple of pairs of sturdy jeans and some T-shirts to fill out the very limited wardrobe she'd brought with her from home.

Nick had finished his business and was reading a newspaper in the lobby when she reached the bank.

He eyed her shopping bags with amusement, then eased himself to his feet carefully, holding his arms close to his side to keep from jarring his ribs. Her mother's shopping trips had been legendary.

"Don't say it," she said before he could speak. "You know I only packed for a weekend. I needed a few things if I'm going to be at the farm much longer."

His lips curved with deepening amusement. "I just was surprised you only had two bags. Somehow I'd expected more."

"Like mother like daughter?" she supplied. "You should know better than that by now."

He surprised her with a quick kiss on the forehead, right there in the middle of the bank lobby. "I do," he said. "I just couldn't resist teasing you."

Dee's jaw dropped, then she narrowed her gaze to focus on the twinkling mischief in his eyes. Teasing? And she'd let it ruffle her. She was slipping. She'd let this morning's incident throw her off balance.

"You're in a good mood," she said, gently taking his arm as they made their way out to the street. "Did your business go well? Or did you swallow half a bottle of those painkillers."

He faked a drug-induced slur and stumble, then winced.

"I guess not. You felt that one," she replied. "So what happened at the bank?"

His enigmatic smile told her nothing, and he refused to divulge anything further.

It was nearly noon when they finished the rest of the errands. As Dee pointed the truck down the highway toward the farm, she wondered just what Nick had planned. The loaded picnic basket sat between them on the bench seat, but he'd rejected her suggestion that they stop at the little park on the edge of town.

"Turn right up here," he ordered, breaking into her thoughts. She cast a questioning glance his way, but his only answer was another secretive smile. He'd been preoccupied since they left the bank with whatever had transpired there. Not that she was complaining. She'd gladly kiss anybody who could put him into a better mood. He'd been grouchier than a bear in the middle of winter for the last few days.

Following Nick's cryptic directions, she drove along the gravel roads until she was completely lost. She only hoped he knew where they were because she was sure she'd never find the way back home on her own. They pulled to a stop in front of a wide, nondescript gate.

"Recognize this?" he asked.

Dee looked around her, then back at him. "No. Should I?" She wondered if she'd just failed some sort of test.

"You will," he said. "I'll open the gate. Drive on through and wait for me."

"I'm not sure," she said. "Whose land is this?"

"I already checked with the owner. He doesn't mind," Nick insisted.

Dee's curiosity mounted. He definitely was up to something. The gate moved easily on well-balanced hinges, so he was able to open it with barely a wince. Shifting the truck into first, she edged through the opening and watched him in the mirrors as he secured the gate behind them. His limp was absent, although the brace he wore probably took much of the stress off his weak ankle.

"Follow this ridge around to that clump of trees," he directed as he climbed back into the cab.

"Is this where we're having our picnic?" she asked.

"I thought you might like the spot."

When Dee halted the truck next to the trees, she understood why. Directly in front of her she recognized the crooked trunk of an ancient sycamore tree. An arching branch hung out over the water, and from there she'd caught her first fish at the age of thirteen.

They were on old man Brown's land. Or at least it used to be. She and Nick would sneak through the back fence and across the fields to the pond up here to catch the giant sunfish that thrived there. That's why she didn't recognize the place before now. She'd never been through the gate or even on that back road.

Dee dragged the picnic basket over to the flat spot beneath a nearby willow, where Nick was already stretched out on the ground, leaning against the trunk. A smug smile warmed his entire face as he watched her.

"You think you're smart, don't you?" she said. "Tricking me with all those turns and side roads until I didn't know where we were."

"We can just go home if you'd rather, but I thought you might enjoy a change of pace."

Dee halted, no longer able to contain her delight. "You thought right. But why couldn't you just tell me. I'd have dressed more appropriately. And I'd have brought a fishing pole."

He shook his head. "Nope. You can fish another day. This is my time."

"Greedy, aren't you? I just spent the last five days devoting myself to your every whim, and you still want more," she teased.

"Wrong," he said. "You've either been working your tail off at the barn or in those flower beds, or you've been sashaying around with Tony doing things he can damn well do for himself."

The hint of resentment in his tone startled her. She narrowed her eyes, studying him. He watched her with undisguised longing, his color high. He wanted her, even now when he was too much in pain to do anything about it. The knowledge brought a familiar tightness to her throat.

He caught her hand and tugged her closer. "Still curious about the bank visit this morning?"

She nodded, puzzled by the sudden intensity in his manner. He seemed restless, as if on the verge of something important. A tingling anticipation sang in her veins at the notion. Her instincts told her that it concerned her.

"It's your business," she said. "But yes, I am curious. You've been on cloud nine since we left the bank."

"I was going to wait until after we ate, but I can't. I'm buying old man Brown's place, most of it, that is. He wants to hold on to the house for a while yet, but he hasn't been able to keep up the rest for a long time. I've been leasing the ground for several years now."

"So we're on your land," she said with a faint, accusing note. He'd let her think they were trespassing, just as he had when they were younger.

"Not officially yet. But I got the loan approval this morning."

She smiled, but something clicked over inside her and died. Another loan, just when he'd paid off Tony's debts.

"How many acres?" she asked.

"Close to three hundred altogether. Some of it's in hay now, some corn. Most of it's good pasture. Clover and timothy. Brown offered it to me a couple of months ago, but it took a while for me to work out the details. It's a complicated arrangement."

He seemed so excited, she couldn't bring herself to dampen his mood. So she pretended to be as happy as he was. But she couldn't see how this could be good for him. If he couldn't afford to stop clowning before, how could he now with this extra loan? Three hundred acres of prime pasture didn't come cheap.

"Have you told Tony yet?"

"He's been in on this all along. He had to be since he's a partner in the horse farm. So what do you think?"

Dee hesitated. She couldn't bring herself to lie. "I'm glad you're happy," was the most tactful thing she could come up with. "Now let's eat. I'm starving."

After a brief hesitation, Nick dropped her hand and reached for the picnic basket. "Let's see now. There's ham sandwiches, ham sandwiches, and ham sandwiches," he said. "No mustard."

She laughed, relieved he hadn't pressed her. "The variety astounds me. I'll take one of each."

They kept the conversation light, playing Remember When until they'd stuffed themselves. The selection really wasn't as limited as he'd indicated, and Dee felt sated and spoiled when they'd finished. He'd included most of her favorites, right down to the slightly warm cheesecake and the grape soda. He'd obviously been planning this for a few days, she decided as she stretched out on the blanket.

Her eyelids refused to stay open, but she couldn't waste this afternoon by sleeping. She pushed herself upright and stretched, trying to wake herself up.

"I'm worse than an old dog," she said when she felt Nick's eyes on her. "I just want to curl up and sleep in the sun." She reached for the picnic basket and started to repack it.

"Forget that," he said, holding out a hand. "Come here. I need to ask you something." His mood had turned serious again. Dee hesitated, not knowing what to expect.

Slowly, she set the dirty paper plates aside and stood. Circling the blanket, she settled herself beside him against the willow trunk.

"So ask," she said as his arm dropped across her shoulders. Then his lips descended on hers in a kiss that was hard and demanding with pent-up need. The feel of it drove all thought, all questions and doubts from her mind as her need matched his, flashing fire to flashing fire.

Just when all rational thought ceased, her fingers slipped under his shirt to touch the rib belt that splinted his broken ribs in place. Stone-cold reason returned to her brain, but her body was much slower to respond.

"Nick—Nick, we can't," she finally managed, pulling away. "You can't. Your ribs."

He wouldn't let her escape. His hands caught hers and he clasped them tightly. "Is that the only reason?"

She glanced at him, puzzled. "What are you talking about?" Had he sensed her unease over the loan? Did he think it was something more?

"I want to touch you," he said, his voice raw and husky. "I want to make love with you until the sun goes down, and then love you again."

Dee held her breath. Or maybe he held it, because she couldn't seem to make her lungs work, or anything else for that matter. "This is crazy," she said. "I don't want to hurt you."

"Then don't," he said. "Love me."

I do, she wanted to say. But she couldn't. Not yet. Not until she was sure he was ready to hear it, until he was ready to make her a permanent part of his life. But he surprised her.

"Love me," he repeated. "Just a tiny bit as much as I love you."

His words caught her by surprise. She hadn't expected them, not yet. But she heard the truth in his low, steady tone.

"I think I always have," she admitted. She didn't touch him yet. The words were enough. The emotion brimming in his eyes said more than she'd ever thought possible. His eyes made promises she was afraid to believe.

But she let herself believe anyway. Just for the moment, she let herself think of forever. Her mind screamed it over and over as she touched him, as she savored the feel of him near her, against her.

"No. Let me," she insisted when he moved over her, hiding his wince at the pain the movement brought. She nudged him backward until he lay flat on the blanket, all bare except for the rib belt. She touched him everywhere she'd dreamed of touching him these last five nights.

They made love slowly, carefully, with infinite gentleness that brought tears to her eyes. He was the one hurt, but he touched her as if she would break. And when he eased back carefully, winching with the sudden protest of the injured ribs, she kissed the pain away and slid over him. Still he caressed her until gentleness was forgotten and the tiny lights exploded inside her head again.

TWELVE

"Do you think you could still freelance from the farm?"

Dee's eyes flew open, all the drowsy, sated sleepiness disappearing with that one question.

"What do you mean? Are you talking about Craig's book? Mom's supposed to bring some of my stuff so I can work on it." When he shifted beside her and trailed insistent fingers down her spine, her eyelids closed and she melted against him.

"Do you need to live in the city, or can you handle things by phone and through the mail?" he asked.

She propped herself up on one elbow and playfully slapped his hand away. "What exactly are you getting at?"

Nick squinted against the sunlight for an instant, then lifted her free hand to his lips. "I don't want you to leave. I wish we could stay here like this forever."

Forever. There was that word again. It frightened him less every time he thought it.

"Me, too," she admitted, looking every bit as wistful as he felt. "But you'll leave again soon."

"You *could* go with me," he suggested.

"Hmm," she said, snuggling against him. "Or you could stay here."

He couldn't, not for much longer. People were depending on him. And he was depending on the money those commitments would bring. He couldn't afford a long recovery that would give rise to rumors that he'd lost his touch or that he was no longer the dependable performer. It wouldn't do him any good, and it wouldn't do the recovering horse business any good, either. No, when he left the circuit for good, he'd do it with pride, not looking like a has-been who's too crippled to work anyway. He didn't think he could make her understand, though. A heavy sigh escaped him as he straightened.

"What's wrong?"

"Nothing. It's getting late. We'd better head back." That much was true. The blanket was mostly in the sun now that the shade had shifted with the afternoon angle of the light. Mostly, though, he needed time to work out things in his mind. He'd lived with this love for years, but only in his mind. The fresh reality of it was still new, and he didn't want to ruin it by moving too fast or forcing either of them to make impossible choices.

Dee's fingers lightly brushed over his sides, skimming over the rib belt before she wrapped her arms gently around him. Her lips briefly touched his shoulder before she rose to her feet and reached for her clothes.

"I think we have too many problems to figure out before we start thinking about forevers. Let's just see how the next couple of weeks go," she said.

Nick nodded and closed his eyes. "If I was sure you'd be happy here, I'd drag you into the nearest church and marry you this minute." He meant it, too. The emotion nearly closed off his throat with its intensity.

"And I might let you," she replied, cupping his face in her hands. "If I was sure you wouldn't get tired of staying in one place."

He let out a long sigh and kissed her palm. "Thank you for that, at least." He hesitated for a moment, then tugged her back down onto her knees until they barely touched.

"I was wondering if you'd consider trying the country out for a while . . ." he began. He touched a finger to her lips as she started to speak. "Don't say anything yet until I finish. I wouldn't want to interfere with your painting. I thought maybe we could find out if there's some kind of compromise that would work. You said you love me. Do you love me enough to try?"

She smiled. "I'm here, aren't I? I could have left that first day on the bus. Or had someone come get me. You didn't really need me here."

Her eyes were warm with love and, unbelievably, bared wanting that still hadn't been sated. "I need you," he replied, and the words hummed along her nerve endings, stirring up new fires.

The afternoon sun was sinking low when the truck reached the Ramsey Ranch drive. As she downshifted, Dee glanced over at Nick and blushed.

"Do you think we can slip inside without Tony spotting us? I'm a mess."

Nick smiled. She looked like a woman who had just been well loved. She had. And despite the nagging ache from his ribs, he felt as if he owned the world. Because she loved him back.

"So what if he does see you?"

"I'm a mess. He's going to take one look at me and start with the teasing. And you know he'll never shut up about it, either."

"What's to worry about? You look beautiful."

"I look like I slept in these clothes."

"You want me to tell him you didn't?"

Her flush deepened, and she shot him a murderous look.

"I guess not," he added, then winced as the truck bounced through a pothole. He made a quick mental note to have more rock dumped on the drive. There were too many holes to drive around.

"Sorry," she muttered as she slowed the truck to ease through another deep one. She sighed, then straightened in her seat as they rounded the last bend in the drive. He followed her gaze out the windshield and drew a deep breath. A shiny white sedan was parked next to the house.

"Mom's here," Dee said, sounding pleased. "I hope she remembered the easel."

"Were you expecting her?" A frisson of unease danced along his spine, then settled like a leaden weight in his stomach. Would the woman try to talk Dee into returning to the city with her?

But Dee seemed oblivious to his sudden concerns. "I knew she'd make it sometime this week. But I figured she'd call first." She parked the truck and tossed the keys to Nick.

"She probably did. We've been gone all day," he reminded her. "How long do you suppose she's been here?"

Dee shrugged. "It's hard to say. She must have gotten away from the office early."

A sparkle lit her eyes when she looked at him. "I'm not buttoned up wrong or something else as telling, am I?"

From the tips of her bare toes to the windblown wisps of her bangs, she was the warm, free-spirited woman who'd made love to him all afternoon. She wore the new clothes she'd bought, not those sophisticated, touch-me-not duds she'd been wearing that morning. And she'd driven with all the windows open and blowing her hair wildly about her.

But it was the warm glow in her eyes, the bruised fullness of her lips that would give her away. The knot of unease untwisted a little. No, he didn't think she'd leave him yet.

"You look pretty well put together," he said.

She rolled her eyes, then got out of the truck and hoisted the picnic basket over the tailgate. He felt odd, letting her assume the burden of the basket, although he had to admit it wasn't that heavy. Even so, his ribs couldn't take much more punishment right now. Not that he'd ever admit as much.

He waited while she sidestepped to peer into the backseat of the white car. She muttered something, then swung the basket around and headed for the house.

"What are you grinning about?" she asked as she drew up beside him on the long, sloping ramp leading to the back porch.

He wasn't about to tell her that his sides ached, that he'd have to take another one of those damned pain pills if he intended to get through the evening without moaning like a sick cow. He didn't want to wipe away the rosy glow, to replace the sated look in her eyes with guilt. *Oh, face it, Ramsey. You're too much of a macho jerk to admit that making love with her jarred the bejesus out of you, in more ways than one.*

"Just wondering what we'll find inside," he said, stopping at the door. It wasn't a lie, either. Although it had been ten years since Pam and Tony had laid eyes on each other, they'd parted in a violent spree of thrown dishes and furious shouts.

"Care to wager on the amount of broken glass in the kitchen?"

Dee grimaced. "Come on. It's been ten years. Look how well we're getting along. Besides, I already warned Mom about the wheelchair, so that shock is out of the way."

"I doubt they've kissed and made up."

Dee stood on tiptoe to place a light peck on his chin. "One miracle per family is enough," she whispered, then reached beyond him for the door handle, leaving him standing alone, smiling at nothing but air.

He caught up with Dee in the hall, where she kicked off her shoes. The house seemed ominously silent. Then he noticed the faint murmur of voices from the kitchen.

"Well, it's about time," Tony called as the two of them stepped into the room. Pam looked up, a startled expression on her face. A strained smile crossed her lips as she greeted her daughter, then began to help unpack the picnic basket.

The tension lay heavy in the sultry heat of the kitchen, and Nick got the distinct impression they'd interrupted an argument. Just like old times.

"I wish I'd known you were coming today. We'd have been home sooner," Dee said in a bright voice. She kissed her mother's cheek then let her fingers drop down to knead the stiff set of Pam's shoulders. Tony looked ready to bend the slotted spoon in his hand around someone's neck, Nick thought. No, he hadn't imagined the tension or the sudden break in the conversation.

"It's nice to see you again, Pamela," he said. "When's supper, Dad?"

"Supper is whenever you get the grill going and put the steaks on," Tony said in a testy tone. "The mushroom sauce is on, and Pam finished the salad half an hour ago. That must have been some picnic. Or did you get lost?''

Nick wasn't sure whether Tony's uncharacteristic bad temper was the result of Pam's arrival or their late return. Probably it was a combination of both. He sent Pam a questioning glance, but the woman just shook her head and gave a little shrug. Dee pursed her lips as her features took on a determined look. Nick decided he didn't want to be around when she began probing for answers.

"I guess that means I'd better hurry with the chores,'' he said.

"And puncture a lung, most likely,'' Dee interjected, marching across the room to jab a pointed finger at his chest. "I promised Pete I'd handle the chores while he was gone and I also promised I'd keep you under control. Now step aside and let me through.''

"Are they always like this?'' Pam asked in a faint voice.

The only answer was a loud snort from Tony, who then wheeled over to the stove and stirred something. "Well, get a move on,'' he said.

"I'll help,'' Nick offered, following her out. "It'll give them a chance to finish their argument.''

"Good point,'' she said, pulling her shoes back on and headed out the door.

Despite his words, or maybe because of them, they hurried through the feeding and watering, doing only the bare minimum that was required. Anything else could wait until morning. Even so, Nick looked tired and drawn by the time they returned to the house.

She changed into a clean blouse and brushed the hay stalks from her hair, then stopped by his room on her way to the kitchen.

"How are the ribs?'' she asked.

He shrugged, setting the prescription bottle on the bedside table without taking any of the painkillers. "Healing just fine," he said, though the lines of strain had returned to his face. "I'll be throwing bales into the loft by Friday. If any of us survive dinner, that is. Do you suppose she's going to drive back tonight or stay over?"

Dee hesitated. "Probably stay over. It's a three-hour trip," she reminded him.

He knew the exact instant the significance of Pam's overnight stay struck Dee. Her smile slipped into a disappointed frown.

"It's probably better anyway that I don't stay with you," she said. "There's your ribs, and then there's Tony. I'd feel kind of strange, sneaking around."

"There's always tomorrow night. And Tony doesn't come up here so there's no reason for him to know anything we don't tell him. Besides, we're adults now," Nick said, easing out off his shirt. He was disappointed, but resigned.

"You're right."

"Tomorrow night?"

"And the next, and the night after that." Her eyes shone with a promise that warmed him. And yet she still seemed to hold something back. He didn't know what, but he knew better than to push. She'd tell him when she was ready, just as she'd told him about her father, and the ex-husband who'd been too stupid to realize his good fortune.

"Then I'll dream about you tonight," he said, letting her see the subdued passion simmering through the faint haze of pain.

Her warm smile was her only answer before she headed downstairs.

Dinner wasn't the ordeal Nick had expected. Throughout the meal, they steered clear of any mention of the past. He was surprised Pam seemed so at ease, considering the tenseness in the kitchen earlier. But she surprised him, and he began to think he must have misjudged her all those years ago.

He remembered her as an angry, selfish woman who held little interest in the farm or its workings. She'd been more concerned with the color of the curtains than the stallion that would bring new blood to the herd. She'd grumbled about the money spent on the stallion, but spent plenty on clothes for herself and her daughter—useless, fancy clothes.

But the woman seated across from him bore little resemblance to the Pamela he'd known then. Nor was she the frumpy housewife who had answered the door in Kansas City. Dressed in some sort of suit, with a silky blouse, she looked expensive and classy. Competent and in control of herself, even if she couldn't control what happened around her. He could easily picture her behind a desk, sorting out the finances and soothing the ruffled feathers of a difficult client.

He understood where Dee had copied her cool, touch-me-not act. Yet he also saw the warmth in Pam's eyes and the faint hint of concern when she looked at her daughter. She wasn't happy Dee was saying here, but she wouldn't interfere. At least not openly. It was the subtle pressure she might apply later that worried him. Somehow he suspected the woman was an expert at subtle manipulation.

As he watched Dee, his fears faded. She wasn't a woman to be easily led. He recognized the stubborn tilt of her head as her mother mentioned the stack of messages accumulating from Dee's answering machine.

"It would help if you could at least tell them when to expect you back," Pam was saying. "As it is, you're probably losing business because you're not available."

Dee shrugged, but Nick could see that the remark hit home. "I'll make a few calls tomorrow," she said. "After I dig through the messages you brought. I suppose Craig's climbing the walls because I'm not working on the book."

"He's afraid you won't finish in time to make the spring list," she said. "You know how he is."

Nick tensed, waiting for Dee's response. "Haven't missed a deadline yet," was all she said before popping a bite of steak in her mouth. The subject appeared closed for the moment, and Nick took advantage of Dee's silence to tell Tony about the bank loan. From there, he managed to steer the conversation in a harmless direction.

Somehow, they all managed to navigate their way through the rough waters without touching any sore points. It wasn't until later that the trouble started. It began with a simple question, and the minute the words left his mouth he wished he could take them back.

"Looks like you've done well for yourself in the last few years," Nick told Pam as they settled into the living room with their coffee.

A dead silence fell on the room. Tony fidgeted uncomfortably with the control panel of his wheelchair while Dee simply glared. He'd meant to compliment the woman on what she'd done with herself since he'd known her before. Instead, it sounded like a double-edged slur aimed at the woman's third marriage and her subsequent higher standard of living.

Oops.

"Dee told me you're a CPA now, a partner in a big firm," he added, trying to redeem himself. Then he remembered. She'd inherited her husband's share of the firm. *Digging it deep now, aren't you, Ramsey?*

"I was a CPA when I married your father," Pam

pointed out. "I gave up a very good job in that firm. And later, they were kind enough to rehire me."

Nick hesitated, thinking before he spoke this time. "I don't believe I ever knew that." No. He would have remembered it, simply because that fact didn't fit with the image he had of his former stepmother.

She shrugged. "It doesn't matter." She really didn't seem to care, and he realized she'd left that part of her life behind her. So what had unsettled her so earlier? It wasn't Tony's physical condition, because Dee said she'd already told her mother about that.

"It matters a heck of a lot," Tony interjected. "Because these two kids have a mistaken idea about why you and I couldn't get along. Considering the present circumstances, it might be a good time to clear the air."

Pam shook her head. "What's done is done. We can't change any of that now. Let it lie. I've learned to, and I thought you had, too."

"I have," Tony said. "I had more than enough time to think and sort things out while I was lying in the hospital bed all those months. But you're wrong about one thing."

Pam tilted her chin at the obstinate angle Nick recognized from watching Dee. "And what might that be?" she said in a deceptively sweet tone.

Tony snorted and wheeled his chair closer to his ex-wife. "Don't get your Irish up, woman. I'm talking about them, not us. In case you haven't noticed, those teenage hormones we used to worry about have come back to haunt us."

Dee groaned and covered her face with her hands. "This is too much," she muttered.

Nick agreed. He wasn't a teenager anymore, although he felt as though he'd drifted back in time as he listened to the older couple's mild argument.

"They should know," Tony insisted. "They have a right to know. It could make all the difference."

"What could make all the difference?" Nick asked. Everyone ignored him. He felt something turn over inside him when the woman took Tony's hand, folding it into her own.

"Perhaps you're right, dear," she said.

Dee appeared as shocked as he was. Shocked speechless, both of them. *What was going on?*

Tony squeezed Pam's hand, then released it.

"Kids, we have a confession to make," Tony began.

Dee frowned impatiently. "If this is about Gloria Winstead or Marla what's-it, I already know. Eleanor Watts, too."

Tony looked nonplussed, and glanced over at Pam.

"She's smart enough to figure it out on her own. She's my daughter, after all," the older woman snapped. "But that's not what we're talking about. Not precisely," she added, turning her attention away from her former husband.

"What we're trying to say is that you kids have a mistaken idea about the reasons our marriage didn't work out," Tony said. "Maybe telling you how it really was will keep the two of you from making the same mistake."

"I'm not that much of your son," Nick retorted, suddenly angry with his father for the assumptions he was making. He'd taken after Tony in a number of ways, but he'd at least kept his head about women, even in his wilder, careless years.

"Watch yourself, boy. You're bordering on being insulting," Tony said mildly. "I'll admit I haven't always been discreet or wise. But our problems started long before Gloria Winstead twitched her butt in my direction."

Dee's grimace mirrored Pam's. "I don't think I want

to hear this,'' Dee said. But she didn't move from her seat.

Pamela left Tony's side and settled onto the arm of the overstuffed chair occupied by her daughter. ''This isn't easy,'' she said, laying her hand on Dee's shoulder. ''When I look at you and Nick, I remember how it was in the beginning with Tony and me.''

''I was charming,'' Tony said with a wink.

Nick released an uneasy laugh. ''Go on,'' he urged.

''Well, we went into the marriage with unrealistic expectations. We were happy at first. Then I got tired of being the little farm wife, and I guess Tony got tired of listening to me. I wasn't too nice to be around, I suppose. Things kind of snowballed from there.''

''Avalanche is more like it,'' Tony interjected with a rueful chuckle. He wheeled closer, stopping his chair between Nick's rocker and the chair where the women sat.

''That doesn't excuse what I did,'' he said, more seriously. ''But how we ended isn't the point. It's how we began. We didn't think everything through clearly. Maybe if Pamela had continued to work, had set up an office in town, she wouldn't have been so unhappy.''

Nick's gaze narrowed. ''So you're trying to warn me not to interfere with Dee's painting—which is unnecessary because I think she's damn good. I don't think the situations really compare. The two of you aren't that much alike. From what I've seen, Dee has always liked the outdoors. Whereas Pam didn't care much for being in the country.''

Pamela shrugged. ''I've never been the outdoor type. And I've never been good at pretending. Maybe that's why I haven't made much of a success of my life outside the office.''

''I wouldn't say that,'' Dee said softly.

''Thanks,'' Pam said, pressing a kiss to her daughter's cheek. "But you always were a bit too loyal to see things clearly. That's what I want you to do now—look at everything clearly before you make any big decisions."

Dee smiled, first at her mother, then at Nick. And in her eyes, he found his reassurance. "Don't worry, Mom. I know what I'm doing. Nick and I were just saying this afternoon that we had a few things to work out yet. We'll manage, whatever happens."

Nick nodded, but deep inside he felt a niggling doubt. Would they really? Or would the farm be too isolated for her to continue her work as before? Would she, like her mother, find that she couldn't live here after all? He hoped not, but the next couple of weeks would tell.

Shouting in the distance teased at Dee's concentration. But it wasn't until Nick hollered from beneath her window that she looked up.

Setting the brush aside, she leaned over the sill, bumping against the screen as she struggled to see what was going on.

"Can you come down to the barn now? I need some help with one of the yearlings," he said.

She hesitated, frowning with irritation at the interruption. She'd spent most of the morning chasing after two calves that had somehow escaped their pen. She and Pete had finally cornered them in a yard half a mile down the road. And yesterday she'd gone with Nick to look at yet another horse he was thinking of buying. She was so far behind, she was beginning to think she might miss the deadline on these illustrations.

"Can you wait a bit? I'm in the middle of something right now." If she could just finish the blue-sky background, she'd be ready for a brief break. She had to change colors to the dusky browns and rusts for the horse then anyway.

He nodded, although that obviously wasn't the answer he'd wanted. "Soon as you can break free," he said, and turned away.

Dee bit her lip, wishing she'd given him a different answer. The careful way he still held his arm told her the ribs still bothered him, particularly this late in the day when he should be resting instead of wrestling with feisty, half-grown horses. She felt faintly guilty for not dropping everything and helping.

Damn, she hated it. Is this how Pamela had felt? Guilty, and then resentful of the guilt, and indirectly, of Tony for making her feel that way? She was beginning to see where their parents had gone wrong. But she wouldn't make the same mistake. She'd talk to Nick tonight, make him understand that these constant interruptions had thrown her dangerously off schedule.

It took longer than she'd expected to finish the background, and by the time she reached the barn it was a full hour later. Nick and Pete were nowhere to be seen.

She searched the outbuildings, then the yard, before locating Tony in a corner of the vegetable garden. He leaned over the edge of his chair, tying a lush tomato plant to its stake. "Taking a break?" he asked when he saw her.

"Looking for Nick. He said he needed help with something."

He thought for a moment, then his expression cleared. "That must have been when he was trying to get that gray filly into the horse trailer. Tom Mitchell from down the road stopped by a bit ago and helped out," he explained. "They've all gone into town now."

She nodded, feeling a sudden coldness that belied the sultry heat of the hot August afternoon. "I didn't realize it would take me so long to finish," she explained. "I should have stopped and helped him." She crossed her arms and wondered why she'd put herself in this impossible position. If she stopped every time Nick thought he needed her, she'd miss her deadline. If she didn't, he'd think she was too much like Pam to fit in. Maybe she was. Maybe she didn't have what it took to make a good farm wife.

"Don't worry yourself about it," Tony said as he tugged the last knot into the strip of torn cloth he'd looped around the tomato stem. "He didn't really need the help. He'd have managed even if Tom hadn't come along. Always did before."

A flash of irritation deepened her frown. "Then why did he bother me with it," she replied. "Never mind, don't answer that. It was probably some kind of test, and I'm really not interested in those kinds of games."

"Naw. The man just misses your company every minute you're away from him. It was that way with your mother and me at first. You'll both simmer down after a while," he said, adding a wicked wink that brought a blush to her cheeks.

She shook her head. "I don't know what's going on inside his head. I suppose he's getting restless," she said before turning away and leaving Tony to his tomatoes. Restless and bored with the farm and with her, she added silently as she made her way back to the house.

Fine, he could be restless. But did he have to interrupt her work because of it? And did she have to feel so left out, so unneeded because he'd managed without her after all? She stomped her way upstairs, muttering about the idiocy of men and the inexplicable workings of their minds—if they truly had them to begin with.

After a while, though, she settled down to work and regained her concentration. She was just finishing the tiny pencil strokes that brought the horse's mane into focus when she heard a tapping at her door.

"Come in," she called without looking up. It had to be Nick. No one else would disturb her up here.

"Sorry," he said as he came through the door. He approached slowly, wearing an uncertain expression. "Tony said you were looking for me. I should have told you we were leaving, but I figured you didn't want to be bothered again."

Her irritation died a quick death as his apology stole the resentment from her before she could give it voice. She shook her head. "Tony talked to you."

Nick nodded. "I shouldn't have bothered you with it in the first place. You've been so busy around this place that you haven't had much time for yourself. I keep forgetting you have your own commitments to meet. Forgive me?"

Dee lifted her head and met his lips halfway. How could she not forgive him when he turned those warm, chocolate-brown eyes on her, when he teased her senses with every touch?

"I'll be finished here in a few minutes," she said when they finally drew apart.

"Don't worry," he said. "Pete and I can handle the chores, and Tony has dinner pretty much in hand. Just do what you have to do and come on down whenever you're ready to."

She stared at his back, feeling like she was hitting the bottom of the roller coaster hill as he left the room and disappeared around the corner. Her lips still burned from the kiss, but the coldness inside her chest was spreading. She tried to tell herself she should be grateful he respected her commitments. He knew she had a job to do, just as he did. Instead, she felt superfluous.

Over the next week, she managed to spend more time helping him on the farm. And by skipping television and working well into the night, she caught up on the sketches somewhat, although not without a price. She missed their quiet evenings together, the twilight walks along the fence line. But she couldn't have it both ways.

It was late one such evening that he appeared in her doorway and waited, watching her silently until she spoke. "Missing me?" she asked, ending with a teasing smile. "I'll be ready for bed in a few minutes."

"Good," he said. "But that's not why I bothered you. Matt just called from Abilene. This new guy isn't working out, and Matt wants me to meet him in Tulsa in a couple of days. I told him I would."

Dee dropped her gaze to the illustration on her easel. The bull was emerging from the chute in a storm of dust and surging muscle. And in a moment, she thought, the clown will jump in and be crushed underfoot once again. She'd feared this moment for weeks. Somehow she'd hoped he'd see the idiocy of returning to the arena.

"You can't go," she said, her voice calm and matter-of-fact.

His eyes widened. "What do you mean I *can't* go? I have to. Matt's depending on me."

"*I'm* depending on you," she argued. "I'm counting on you to keep yourself in one piece until we figure out whether we have something worth keeping here."

"I think we do. In fact, I'm sure," he said.

She hesitated, then looked away.

"Dee?"

"I thought I was," she said. "But now—"

One gentle, calloused finger on her lips stopped her. "Don't say it," he said.

She kissed the finger. "Your ribs are in no shape for this. You can't yet. I can't watch you do this."

He shook his head. "You don't have to. I thought

you might want me to drop you off in Kansas City so you can wrap up a few things."

She considered that for a moment. "Kansas City isn't on the way to Tulsa," she commented.

"I'm going to be gone for a while. We're booked solid until the first week of December," he said.

She stepped back without a word. So this was it. The end. And it had slipped up on her unawares. Unwilling to let him see the tears misting her eyes, she turned away and fumbled with the brushes. She blinked hard and began putting her supplies away.

His hands touched her shoulders. "Think about it. Get used to the idea of me going back to clowning. Because it seems as though you've been kidding yourself that we'd live happily ever after here on the farm, you with your paints and me with my horses. But those rodeos, those bulls, and that crazy face I paint on are what pays for this place now. That's how we paid for the new roof on the barn and those yearlings out in the pasture."

Dee drew in a deep breath. "How much longer, Nick? How many horses, how much land do you have to buy before you can quit? Why can't you borrow the money or take on a partner instead? Hell, I'd lend you the money. I'd give it to you if you'd just take care of yourself." She twisted around as she spoke, taking in his rising anger, his frustration at her failure to back up his decision.

"The doctor said six weeks," she continued.

Nick shrugged. "That's most people. I'm in a lot better shape than most people. I only stayed out three weeks last time."

"Last time?"

"Hell, I didn't want to tell you, but yes, last time I had a busted rib I was back to work with Matt in three weeks. I guess he figured I'd be ready or he wouldn't have called tonight."

"And the ankle? It's not in such good shape, either. Damn it, Nick. Why are you doing this?"

He held her gaze with eyes that didn't waver in intensity. "Commitments. People depend on me, riders, stock contractors, Matt. I can't let them down. You should understand that. I agreed to do a job, and I have to do it."

"No matter what the cost?"

Nick's hands cupped her face. "I know it was hard for you to see what happened up there in Iowa. But I can't let one accident stop me from doing what I do best. There's no guarantee I won't get hit by a truck the next time I cross the street. Life's a bunch of risks, and clowning is no bigger a risk than most anything else, considering the know-how I've accumulated over the years."

Dee nodded slowly. "I suppose I can understand that. Just don't expect me to watch. And don't expect me to wait at the gate for you. That's asking too much."

His fingers trailed down her cheek to caress her neck. "I know what I'm doing," he said, trying to reassure her. He didn't know how to wipe away the fear in her eyes.

"Sure, Nick." She slipped out of his arms and returned to the easel.

He wanted to pull her back, crush her against him. She was slipping away from him, shutting herself away. He touched her, and she stiffened. Slowly, he pulled his hand back.

"I guess I'd better pack," she said in a lifeless tone. "You'll want to get an early start in the morning."

He didn't answer. He couldn't. He slammed the door closed behind him when he left the room, then fell back against the wall and squeezed his eyes closed tight as he fought the urge to scream.

He had to make things right. He'd find a way.

He drew a deep, calming breath and walked into his room, closing the door softly behind him.

THIRTEEN

Dee carefully replaced the receiver and stared at the silent phone for a long moment. Her heart thumped heavily in her chest, but she couldn't stave off the inevitable depression that always took hold the minute the dial tone replaced Nick's voice on the telephone line.

She'd been home for two months and she hadn't seen him once in all that time. He'd called from Tulsa, and from Houston and a dozen other places she'd never heard of. Two or three times a week he called. He never said what she needed to know. He just told her where he'd be next, who he'd seen, and what prizes his horses had helped various cowboys claim.

He never said he loved her. Not anymore. So she didn't say it, either.

The doorbell chimed when she was halfway up the stairs. She hesitated, tempted to ignore it. She didn't feel like talking to anyone, least of all a kid selling magazines or one of her kindly but nosy neighbors. However, when the visitor leaned on the bell, she changed her mind and trudged back downstairs.

She opened the door to find Craig, holding up a frosty bottle.

"Dust off the champagne glasses, Dee. We're celebrating." He pushed past her and disappeared down the hallway into the kitchen, leaving her standing at the open door.

Sighing, she latched it, then followed the sound of the cork popping. "What's the occasion? Did Mom finally give in?"

A wry smile crossed his lips. "You think I'd be drinking champagne with you?"

"Well, as a co-conspirator I have certain privileges."

Craig snorted. "Those privileges extend to giving the bride away and that's it. Not that there appears to be any such nonsense in the offing," he added, shooting her a glance.

"Don't look at me," she said, forcing a nonchalant shrug. She'd actually thought for a while in those terms, but as the weeks passed, she'd been forced to face reality. Nick was not going to be a permanent fixture in her future. At best, he'd remain on the fringes for a while, but the calls would eventually taper off.

"Nope," Craig continued. "We're celebrating the acceptance of the best book I've done yet," he said, pouring the bubbly liquid into two coffee cups. The faint slur to his words indicated he'd already been celebrating for a while.

"Congratulations," she said.

"Cheer up," he said. "This is a party. They're tickled pink with your illustrations. So they'll be sending lots more your way, and not just for my books, either, I'll bet. You could be doing the jacket art for their new line of westerns they're talking about starting—oops, that's confidential. Pretend you didn't hear that." His lopsided grin indicated he was already slightly inebriated.

She wished she could share his enthusiasm. She was happy for him, and of course she'd rather be doing cover art than laundry detergent ads. But it all seemed so pointless and empty. It didn't mean anything, not like it used to.

She took a sip of the champagne, then drained the cup quickly and held it out for more. Even if she felt like the bottom of a worn shoe, she didn't have to act like it. She could at least pretend a little enthusiasm.

"To us," she said, holding up the cup.

"To us," Craig repeated. "We make a great team." His words had a hollow ring to them. He tipped the cup back and gulped down the entire contents.

"Ahh, much better," he said when he had finished. "Nothing like a little cheap champagne. Even if I am drinking it with the wrong lady."

Dee sighed as the gaity left him. She realized then it had been forced all along, only she'd been too preoccupied to notice. Now, his forlorn expression mirrored her own feelings.

"Why don't you call Mom? Take her to lunch?" she suggested.

"She's in a meeting all morning. She has a luncheon speech with the Business Women's Association, followed by a long session sorting out a bankruptcy. Maybe I should take her secretary to lunch. I talk to her more than Pam anyway."

"Mom's a fool."

"No, my girl. She's cautious of committing herself a fourth time. She cares. It's just that I want more than she's able to give. It's about time I accepted that."

Dee forced a smile. "Well, you have your book to console you. I'm happy for you. For us."

Craig's graying brows drew together in a deepening frown. "Can the act, Melody Williams. If you were any gloomier, you'd be wailing and tearing at your clothes. Nick hasn't called lately, has he?" It was more of a supposition than a question.

She sighed heavily. "Wrong. I talked to him a minute ago."

"He's still risking his neck."

She nodded. "I guess it was silly of me to expect him to stop just because I asked him to. And just because the doctor and anybody else with half a brain thinks he'll cripple himself." Her frown deepened. Nick was so damned stubborn. He'd set himself on a course to rebuild the family farm, and he'd nearly succeeded in restoring it to its former prosperity. But he didn't know when to stop.

"So forget about him," Craig suggested.

"I should," she agreed, setting the cup aside. "I really should."

"You don't need him. You don't need the hassle or the distractions, not when your career as an artist is ready to take off."

She held up a protesting hand. "An illustrator. I'm too damned practical to be a real artist."

Craig slammed his cup down, spilling some of the liquid on the countertop. "That's your damned ex-husband talking, not you. Granted, he did some creative stuff, but a life-size sculpture of teenagers in the backseat doesn't have many practical applications—except of course as a marital aid for anyone interested in new positions." He added a lascivious wink, then propped his elbow in the spill. "What a mess. Where do you hide the paper towels?"

Dee tossed him the roll from the rack by the stove. She didn't want to think about David, or Nick, either, especially in the same breath. There was no comparison. David had been carefree, amoral, selfish, and utterly charming in spite of his faults. He was what he was, and there was no changing him.

Nick had his own sort of charm, but he was more grounded and practical. He was dependable, the kind of man with an aura of excitement, or risk and danger about him. He was responsible, in every way except his own well-being, and that's what disturbed her. She couldn't tolerate the constant risk, the ever-present fear that the next time he wouldn't escape with just a few broken bones. And it didn't appear he had any intention of changing.

Maybe that was the problem. She'd expected him to. Just like she'd expected David to change. She hadn't accepted either of them as they were. In the scope of things, Nick wasn't so far from perfect. Maybe she was the fool.

Craig's triumphant laugh startled her out of her thoughts. "I knew there had to be some here someplace," he said, pulling a wine bottle from the back of the refrigerator.

"Don't you think you've had enough?"

Craig shook his head. "Not nearly enough. How about you? Feel like forgetting for a while? We could get sloshed and sing silly songs."

She grinned. "Come on up to the studio. I'll show you what a practical artist can do with peanut butter."

Craig sputtered, looking nonplussed. "Peanut butter, you said?"

"Yeah," she said, grabbing the bottle by the neck and turning away. "I'm working on the art for a new ad campaign. It's big bucks if the agency's client likes it."

More money now meant more time later to work on something she enjoyed, like the painting sitting on her easel right now. It wasn't something that would bring her a lot of money, but hanging on the landing, it would make her happy.

"I'll bring the corkscrew," he offered. "We'll finish the champagne, then start on the vino. And after that?"

"You go home in a taxi," she called from the landing.

She didn't work on the peanut butter ad after all. She went to bed to sleep off all the wine and champagne. Craig had long since collapsed on the couch downstairs.

The jangling of the phone awoke her sometime later, but she didn't reach it until after the machine picked up. She stood next to her easel, one hand to her throbbing head and the other braced on the drafting table, listening to Nick's message. She sank onto the floor and burst into tears.

"Damn him," she muttered, weakly pounding the wooden floor and repeating it until she didn't have the energy to even sit up. Then she replayed the message.

"I was hoping you'd be there," he said in a voice that sounded tired and strained. "I got a hold of a couple of passes to the Kansas City Royal Rodeo. Our schedule's so tight I won't be able to see you before then. Anyway, I'll call again so we can make plans."

She listened to it three times before she plunked the tape out of the machine and threw it into the trash. His words weren't the problem. It was the noise in the background, the faint sound of sirens, muffled voices and frantic footsteps, and the damning voice over the loudspeaker paging a Dr. Johnson. Nick was in a hospital. Again.

Nick was hurt, yet his message indicated he had every intention of continuing this madness. She couldn't be a part of it, not in any sense. She obviously couldn't change his mind. So she had to erase him from hers—or go crazy from worry.

It took Dee only fifteen minutes to remove every trace of him from her studio. She packed all the preliminary sketches and the few finished watercolors into a box and put them into the attic. The photos from the rodeo in Benton were delegated to a bottom drawer. Then she stood on a chair and ripped the sketches of Nick himself from the wall. Those she tucked away in the back of a cabinet. She couldn't bring herself to destroy them, but she couldn't look at them anymore. It was over.

She screened all her calls with the answering machine. But the calls from Nick didn't stop until after Pam answered one day and explained why her daughter refused to speak to him.

The passes arrived a few days later, wrapped in a blank sheet of paper. There was no message and no return address.

She finished the peanut butter ad, then illustrated an Easter story for a local children's magazine. After that, she cleaned her studio. In the second hour of scrubbing and polishing, she found the photo.

It had slipped down between the cabinet and the drafting table. A single look undid everything she'd tried to accomplish. The memories flooded over her in a warm, hazy blanket that brought a smile to her lips, the first in days.

She tacked the picture onto the wall above her easel, then pulled out her paints and brushes. She'd been a fool to try to forget. She'd never found peace that way. She'd found it in her painting.

So she painted.

Pam couldn't see what was so fascinating about a stupid cat clinging to a galloping horse's tail. Craig had only shrugged, then dragged Pam off to the symphony one night, dinner another, and eventually the bedroom, Dee suspected. She wasn't sure because she'd closed the studio door, shutting out the soft whispers and quiet laughter.

She ignored the phone, the calendar, the tickets, and anything that threatened to draw her attention away from the painting. It wasn't until one evening when she happened through the kitchen in search of food that she noticed something of the outside world.

The television blared out the day's news while Pam chopped vegetables and Craig hovered about, more in the way than helping. The man pinched her mother on the behind, and then she smiled at him.

Dee blinked, then turned away. Things were looking up in that direction. They'd been a threesome before, with Craig more in the position of Dee's friend than Pam's date. Dee's preoccupation seemed to have changed that. She was glad something good was coming from it.

Quickly she made herself a sandwich, trying to ignore the low whispers that intermingled with the drone of the newscaster's voice. She turned to leave, glancing discreetly away from the older couple.

As she passed by, she caught a glimpse of a familiar face on the television screen.

She watched as Nick and Matt, both dressed in full cowboy clown regalia, rounded a hospital bed and chatted with a small boy who was recovering from heart surgery. Her own heart swelled in her chest until she thought she would burst from the flooding emotion.

The low buzz of young voices filled Kemper Arena when she arrived, but Dee barely noticed the sea of blue jackets from the Future Farmers of America. Her attention was focused on her twisting fingers rather than the youthful faces around her. She wasn't sure why she'd come or what she expected to accomplish this afternoon. Last night it had seemed like the right thing to do. Now she wasn't so sure.

She'd dithered around so long getting ready that she arrived halfway through the second event, missing the first heat of bull riders altogether. That meant she'd probably wait more than an hour for another chance to see Nick. She tried to relax while the trick rider entertained the crowd, and while the tight-turning horses raced around the barrels and the ropers snagged their calves—or missed. But she kept scanning the chutes, hoping for a glimpse of him among the watching cowboys back there.

Finally, it was time for the last heat of bull riders—the last event of the rodeo. The bulls snorted and thumped against the metal bars of the chutes. Then the clowns came out, and she lost track of anything else. Her throat tightened as Nick rolled the padded barrel out to the center of the arena, then launched into a shouting match with his partner. Matt, still sporting his strangely colored wig, matched him insult for insult until a third clown joined the fray.

The words were lost on her. She simply drank in the sight of Nick's painted face. Just seeing him brought a heaviness to her chest, a physical manifestation of the regrets that taunted her every waking moment. Then a word from the announcer diverted the attention back to the chutes, where a rider was climbing on.

She leaned forward in her seat as the clowns took their places. She blinked twice, then a soft smile stole on to her lips as Matt moved closer to the chutes, while Nick stood behind the barrel, some forty feet back.

She steeled herself, knowing what to expect but already playing over in her mind the accident that had broken Nick's ribs. The gate swung open and the heavy bell jangled as the bull bucked and twisted. She clenched her eyes closed. She kept them that way until the loud buzzer signaled the end of the ride. A moment later, the bull was out of the arena and nobody had been hurt. Nick walked over and slapped the rider on the back, moving with rolling grace that ended with a slight hitch on the left side. His bad ankle. She felt the nausea rise from her stomach. He'd taken the less dangerous role. But even from here, she could see his ankle wasn't up to snuff.

"Excuse me," she whispered, rising and pushing past four bewildered boys before they had a chance to move their long legs out of the way.

She practically ran down the wide corridor that ringed the arena's seating area. Once she reached the exits, she pushed open a door and rushed outside.

The chill air cooled her skin, easing the nausea. But it didn't ease her fears. Leaning against a pillar, she closed her eyes and breathed in deeply, trying to calm her racing heart. Then the imprint of Nick's painted face, of the rolling walk, flashed through her mind. A frisson of excitement danced up her spine.

She couldn't leave, not yet. In spite of it all, she had to see him, touch him, and tell him how wrong she'd been to expect him to change. She couldn't change him, any more than she could change the color of the sky.

Moving slowly, she turned back to the doors, then hesitated. If she wanted to talk to him, she wouldn't be able to accomplish it by returning to her seat. Instead, she surveyed the grounds, searching for another entrance. She followed a wide set of stairs down to the street level and headed for the covered strip where several riders were walking their horses to cool them down.

Working her way carefully, she slipped through the wide opening that led down into the bowels of the arena. While her eyes adjusted to the dimness, she stepped over to the wall and surveyed the surroundings. She was somewhere behind the chutes. She wandered around for a moment, trying to figure out where Nick would come out when the bull rides were finished.

That's when she spotted Freda. She tugged gently on her horse's reins and led it over to where Dee waited.

"You're the last person I expected to see around here," Freda commented as she drew close.

Dee nodded, not knowing how to begin. "I guess I'm a little surprised myself," she admitted. "I'm looking for Nick."

Freda grinned. "About time. Come on with me," she said, tossing her reins to a stocky man in a black Stetson. She grabbed Dee's hand, pulling her along before she had a chance to ask where. "Hurry up. There isn't much time before the bull riding's finished, and I think it would be better if you could meet him someplace private."

She led Dee through a set of double doors that swished closed beyond them, shutting out the earthy smells and muting the cheers of the audience. Freda's boots clicked on the tiled floor as she hurried down the wide corridor, then stopped in front of a metal door.

"This is it. You can wait for him here," she said. "I'll pass the word on to Matt to leave you two alone for a while to work things out."

Dee clasped Freda's hands in her own. "Thanks, but I don't think it's possible. I've waited too long. I just don't want him to hate me, that's all. I couldn't stand that," she said, her voice breaking at the end.

Freda sniffed, then dropped Dee's hands and hugged her. "Break a leg, kid. Preferably his," she said. "That might buy you enough time to knock some sense into him. And when you're finished, you can tell me how it's done."

Another cheer filtered through the walls and doors, and Freda pulled away, smiling mistily. "One more bull and the guys will be back this way."

"You're sure. Maybe he'll stay out there or go straight to the trailer."

Freda shook her head. "He's not been much for hanging out with the boys lately. He'd rather be on his own. Besides, his gear is here."

Dee nodded and watched Freda until she disappeared from sight. Then she turned to the door labeled as the clowns' dressing room and opened it.

Three snack machines and a scattering of gear filled the small space. Matt's infamous hot-pink bra lay over the back of the only chair. She picked it up, thinking to toss it aside and accidentally tripped the squeeker. But for once she couldn't summon up a hint of amusement, because on the chair seat was Nick's opened makeup case, with her photograph taped inside the lid.

Her fingers flew to her throat as she gasped. She didn't know where he'd gotten that particular picture. It was a recent one, a snapshot taken at the Benton Arena from what she could guess. Before she could touch it, the door opened behind her.

Jerking upright, she spun around as Nick entered. His eyes widened with surprise when he saw her standing there with that ridiculous pink thing in her hand.

"I didn't expect to see you here," he commented. His nonchalant tone struck her heart like a whip. She'd expected anger or maybe even forgiveness—but not this cold indifference.

"You sent me the tickets," she said, throwing out the words like a challenge.

He shrugged. "I didn't know you'd gotten them. I haven't talked to you in a while." He turned away and fumbled with his shoe lacings. He wore some sort of brace on his ankle, which explained why he'd taken the lesser role as barrel man. But at least he'd compromised that much.

She lifted her chin and surveyed him from head to toe, then back again. Out in the arena, he had seemed alive with energy. He'd looked the part of the mischievous clown. Now his every movement reflected fatigue. When he set aside the makeup case and settled into the chair, the harsh lighting revealed new lines of strain around his eyes.

He wore the same oversize cut-off overalls he'd worn that night in Benton when he'd kissed her and touched the half-moon scar on her forehead. She closed her eyes remembering.

"Why wouldn't you talk to me?" he asked, barely above a whisper.

She leaned back against the concrete walk, concentrating on the rough coolness that penetrated the soft warmth of her sweater. Then she opened her eyes and met his hurt gaze.

"You were in the hospital. When I listened to the message on the answering machine, all those hospital noises in the background scared me. I wasn't ready to live with the constant fear of you being injured again."

His brows drew together in puzzlement. "What are you talking about? I haven't been inside a hospital for months, except for a couple of times that I stopped in to visit a guy who'd been hurt pretty badly out in Wyoming."

"I heard somebody paging a doctor?"

He shook his head helplessly, then comprehension dawned across his features. "I guess I did use the pay phone there once. What does that have to do with anything?"

"What's that on your leg?" she asked, answering his question with one of her own.

"This?" he asked, indicating the brace. "It's nothing. I had some tendon damage from the fall I took in Iowa. This just gives the ankle a little extra support."

"Should you even be bullfighting?"

An angry frown twisted his painted-on smile. "Despite your doom and gloom predictions, I wasn't in the hospital because of this ankle or any other injury.'' He pulled a bottle from the makeup case and began smearing baby oil on his face, smearing the colors.

''So tell me about this brace,'' Dee retorted. ''It's not the one you wore at the farm.''

Nick hesitated, then heaved a sigh. ''It's similar. This one's custom-made. It gives better support, and it's more flexible than my old one. It's what keeps me from ripping what's left of the tendons loose until I have the surgery,'' he explained, then reached for a towel to wipe away the smears.

Her breath stopped. Surgery, he'd said. She didn't know whether she was more angry that he was risking further damage to the ankle or relieved that he'd finally listened to the doctors.

''When did you decide this?'' she asked, stepping closer.

''The day before I brought you back to Kansas City,'' he snapped back. He flung the towel into the case and snapped the lid shut.

''And you didn't tell me? You let me worry for two months about whether you'd cripple yourself. That was mean, Nick. Selfish and mean. I'd never have thought that of you.'' By the time she finished speaking, she was inches from touching him.

''I never thought *you* would shut me out without so much as an explanation or a Dear John note,'' he retorted. The hurt she'd caused him was evident, and suddenly the anger drained out of her, leaving her tired and empty.

''I'm sorry. It just seemed like the best thing to do at the time,'' she said. ''I couldn't change your mind about bullfighting. And I couldn't settle for a stubborn rodeo clown who doesn't know when to stop. Heck, I didn't even know you could slow down until I saw you working the barrel a little while ago.''

His hand reached out to cup her cheek. "I had things to take care of before I could talk to you. I wanted to drag you into the nearest church and marry you, but I had to come to you free and clear with no complications and no loose ends. I guess I just waited too long," he said with a catch in his voice. "Or maybe I was just kidding myself that you cared enough to settle for a horse farmer."

She shook her head. "Don't ever think that. I care too much to watch you keep hurting yourself this way. It was tearing me up. I thought I had to forget you or go crazy."

"So why did you come today?"

"I was just going to watch the rodeo and then go home. I wanted to see for myself that you were all right. But I couldn't even watch. I made a fool of myself, practically crawling over those kids to get away. Then I found I couldn't leave, not without talking to you and apologizing for the way I treated you."

"You hurt me," he said.

Her eyes misted. "I know. I'm sorry I didn't understand. I shouldn't have tried to change you. I should have known better this time."

"This time?" he asked, tugging her closer. With one sharp jerk, he pulled her resisting body into his lap.

"We have to talk," she said, trying to pull away. "I need to explain."

"Later. Right now I just want to hold you."

She felt the tremor in his body as he pulled her against him, hugging her close with an intensity bordering on desperation.

For a moment, she couldn't move. Then her body slowly relaxed, molding itself to his shape. "I thought I could make David change, but he didn't. I tried to make you change, but that wasn't fair. I guess now I'm ready to accept you as you are. I just hope I'm not too late."

She nuzzled closer, pressing a kiss to his neck.

"Don't do that," he said.

Dee stiffened, pulling herself away as hurt and confusion flooded her. But he wouldn't let her escape completely. She turned her face away, hoping he wouldn't see the lone tear that slid down her cheek. She'd laid herself bare, and he'd rejected her. She didn't want him to know how deeply that hurt. Yet he did.

"Oh, Dee—don't," he said softly, brushing the tear away with a calloused thumb. He kissed the spot reverently. His gentle caring reminded her of the times he'd comforted her years ago. That brand of comfort only deepened the pain.

"I'm sorry I bothered you," she said, trying to rise.

"If you don't stop wriggling around, I'm going to lose what little restraint I have left," he said in a strained voice. "I love you, and when you touch me like that, I want to pull you right down onto the floor." He pulled her hard against him, letting her feel how close he was to losing control.

She felt a hot flush rise as he pressed himself against her. He desired her, and he cared enough to comfort her. "Then do it," she whispered. "Lock the door and make love to me."

He shook his head. "Not now. Not here. And not until we settle a few things."

"Such as?" She undid his top shirt button.

He rebuttoned it. "Such as whether you're going to marry me."

"Name the date."

"And where we're going to live."

"At the farm." She popped one of his bright red suspenders loose.

He caught her hands before she could undo anything else. "You'll miss the city," he said.

"I won't."

"Keep your house. You can go there whenever you need to be closer to your clients and when you want to go to the ballet, or the symphony, or whatever. Besides, Pam still needs a place to live."

She shrugged. "I'll concede that point, if you'll agree to cut back on your bullfighting schedule. I'm not suggesting you quit altogether, although that's what I'd really like. But you'll be laid up for a while after the surgery, and you also need to spend more time at the farm if you're going to make a success of it. And I can help with that."

Nick pressed a hard kiss to her lips. "Done."

"Good," she replied, brushing teasingly against his lips until he groaned and responded with a sweet, compelling urgency that rocked her senses.

"Stand up," he whispered.

"What!"

He eased her off his lap, then stood beside her. Dropping a kiss on her nose, he pulled her to the door.

"Where are you going?"

"We're leaving, before anybody else shows up," he said. "I know of a trailer where we can have a little more privacy, a little more comfort . . ."

"Nick, you can't—"

He turned and pulled her back into the warmth of his arms, his lips teasing kisses along her nape. "Why not?"

"Your shoes," she managed to whisper before his lips closed over hers.

A soft knock at the door, followed by a louder one interrupted the kiss before it could spiral out of control. The door swung open to reveal Matt and Freda, both grinning like conspirators.

"It worked," Matt said, hugging the woman beside him. "I'm losing a partner, but it looks like I might get my best friend back."

Dee straightened, pulling at her clothing and blushing at the button that had come undone without her knowing it. "What's he talking about?" she asked Nick.

"I think he means I've been a bit moody lately."

"Moody?" Freda squealed. "He's been worse than the devil himself."

"Yeah, that's why we had to put him in the barrel. No self-respecting bull would go near him. He was scaring them clean out of the arena with that frown of his," Matt added.

Freda rolled her eyes and moved out of the circle of Matt's arms. "He exaggerates."

"No. I mean the part about losing a partner," Dee demanded.

"He hasn't told you?"

"I hadn't gotten to that part yet," Nick explained. "But since you brought the subject up, this is my last rodeo for a while. Matt's found somebody to fill in for me for the next few months at least, maybe permanently. I'm not sure how long it will take this ankle to heal after the surgery."

Dee pinched his bare forearm, then darted away before he could grab her. "You could have told me sooner," she retorted, trying to sound angry. She utterly failed, thanks to the heart-felt relief flooding her.

He reached out to pull her back, but she eluded his grasp. "I wanted to. But I had to know whether you really loved me enough to take me as I am, warts and bullfighting and all."

She managed a faint frown. "I feel like a fool."

He shook his head. "You look like my idea of heaven," he said.

Matt cleared his throat. "Much as I hate to break up this little party, we have an appointment with a certain man who could be very influential to our career—well, *mine* now, I guess. I'd like to keep him happy so he'll send more bookings my way."

Nick nodded. "You go on ahead."

Matt shook his head. "He's expecting you, too."

"All right," he said, turning to Dee. "I'll make my excuses in person. Will you wait for me here? I promise I'll only be a few minutes."

"I'll wait." She'd wait forever, if that's what it took.

But after the others had left, she grew restless in the tiny room, and stepped out into the corridor. Five minutes turned into ten, and then into fifteen, and she began to consider searching him out.

Then Nick entered through a side door, spotted Dee, and ran toward her.

"Come on," he said, leading the way toward the exit.

"What about your things?"

"Matt will bring them later."

She took his hand and followed him. "So where are we going?"

"I believe you mentioned something about making love, and the floor, and marriage, not necessarily in that order."

She laughed. "Some of that was your idea."

"Yeah," he said, stopping and pulling her behind a convenient pillar. "You're mine. You always have been."

"In my heart," she admitted.

"Kiss me," he ordered, swinging her into his arms.

Dee clung to him, pouring all the passion and love

she felt into the kiss. When their lips parted, she smiled mistily.

"I love you, Nick Ramsey," she said.

"You'd better," he said. "Because I don't like the idea of being in love alone anymore."

"Not a chance," she said, pressing her lips to his once again.

SHARE THE FUN . . .
SHARE YOUR NEW-FOUND TREASURE!!

You don't want to let your new books out of your sight? That's okay. Your friends can get their own. Order below.

No. 22 NEVER LET GO by Laura Phillips
Ryan has a big dilemma. Kelly is the answer to *all* his prayers.

No. 40 CATCH A RISING STAR by Laura Phillips
Justin is seeking fame; Beth helps him find something more important.

No. 78 TO LOVE A COWBOY by Laura Phillips
Dee is the dark-haired beauty that sends Nick reeling back to the past.

No. 21 THAT JAMES BOY by Lois Faye Dyer
Jesse believes in love at first sight. Will he convince Sarah?

No. 23 A PERFECT MATCH by Susan Combs
Ross can keep Emily safe but can he save himself from Emily?

No. 24 REMEMBER MY LOVE by Pamela Macaluso
Will Max ever remember the special love he and Deanna shared?

No. 25 LOVE WITH INTEREST by Darcy Rice
Stephanie & Elliot find $47,000,000 *plus* interest—true love!

No. 26 NEVER A BRIDE by Leanne Banks
The last thing Cassie wanted was a relationship. Joshua had other ideas.

No. 27 GOLDILOCKS by Judy Christenberry
David and Susan join forces and get tangled in their own web.

No. 28 SEASON OF THE HEART by Ann Hammond
Can Lane and Maggie's newfound feelings stand the test of time?

No. 29 FOSTER LOVE by Janis Reams Hudson
Morgan comes home to claim his children but Sarah claims his heart.

No. 30 REMEMBER THE NIGHT by Sally Falcon
Joanna throws caution to the wind. Is Nathan fantasy or reality?

No. 31 WINGS OF LOVE by Linda Windsor
Mac & Kelly soar to new heights of ecstasy. Are they ready?

No. 32 SWEET LAND OF LIBERTY by Ellen Kelly
Brock has a secret and Liberty's freedom could be in serious jeopardy!

No. 33 A TOUCH OF LOVE by Patricia Hagan
Kelly seeks peace and quiet and finds paradise in Mike's arms.

No. 34 NO EASY TASK by Chloe Summers
Hunter is wary when Doone delivers a package that will change his life.

No. 35 DIAMOND ON ICE by Lacey Dancer
Diana could melt even the coldest of hearts. Jason hasn't a chance.

No. 36 DADDY'S GIRL by Janice Kaiser
Slade wants more than Andrea is willing to give. Who wins?

No. 37 ROSES by Caitlin Randall
It's an inside job & K.C. helps Brett find more than the thief!

No. 38 HEARTS COLLIDE by Ann Patrick
Matthew finds big trouble and it's spelled P-a-u-l-a.

No. 39 QUINN'S INHERITANCE by Judi Lind
Gabe and Quinn share an inheritance and find an even greater fortune.

No. 41 SPIDER'S WEB by Allie Jordan
Silvia's quiet life explodes when Fletcher shows up on her doorstep.

No. 42 TRUE COLORS by Dixie DuBois
Julian helps Nikki find herself again but will she have room for him?

No. 43 DUET by Patricia Collinge
Adam & Marina fit together like two perfect parts of a puzzle!

Meteor Publishing Corporation
Dept. 292, P. O. Box 41820, Philadelphia, PA 19101-9828

Please send the books I've indicated below. Check or money order only—no cash, stamps or C.O.D.s (PA residents, add 6% sales tax). I am enclosing $2.95 plus 75¢ handling fee for *each* book ordered.

Total Amount Enclosed: $________.

____ No. 22	____ No. 25	____ No. 31	____ No. 37
____ No. 40	____ No. 26	____ No. 32	____ No. 38
____ No. 78	____ No. 27	____ No. 33	____ No. 39
____ No. 21	____ No. 28	____ No. 34	____ No. 41
____ No. 23	____ No. 29	____ No. 35	____ No. 42
____ No. 24	____ No. 30	____ No. 36	____ No. 43

Please Print:
Name ______________________________
Address ______________________ Apt. No. ________
City/State ____________________ Zip ________

Allow four to six weeks for delivery. Quantities limited.